THE ILLUSTRATED STORY-TELLER.

THE SPANISH GIPSEY.

LONDON: W. S. JOHNSON, 60, ST. MARTIN'S LANE, CHARING CROSS.

TO BE HAD OF ALL BOOKSELLERS.

THE SPANISH GIPSY.

CHAPTER I.

The days of the gipsy power in Spain—Midnight and a sleeping city—The three robbers—The young prisoner—Influence of freedom and a roving life—The superstitious guard.

"No washing will turn the gipsy white."—FERDOUSI.

OUR story opens at that period of Spanish history when it most resembled romance—the latter half of the sixteenth century, when roving bands of gipsys were the virtual masters of the country, being so well organised and numerous as to dispute the power of the law, and to place the troops of the king at defiance. A period when a belligerent spirit seemed to pervade the atmosphere—when a man's hands were often raised against his brother—when civil wars frequently distracted the entire country—and when each man was educated to the profession of arms, because no one knew how soon he might be called upon to enact the soldier.

The city of Logrono, chief town of the province of Rioja, bordering on Arragon, is the spot where we would first introduce the reader, and to the family of Alvarez, one of the proud old Castilian names that had held precedence in the land for centuries, but whose fortunes had been lessened, and whose numbers decreased by fierce battles with the swarthy Moors on the plains of Arragon. Francisco Alvarez was the present representative of the house; a noble cavalier, whose heart knew no debasing quality, and who had inherited a daring and chivalrous spirit from his birth. He was still rich in the inheritance of his father's estates, and his house showed, in its half Moorish style of architecture, so broad and massive in extent, and so secure and impregnable in detail, that its master lived like a prince, and was fully prepared to defend his own.

It is of the fortunes of Don Francisco, in part, that these pages will treat.

It was the calm summer season of the year, and the hour was nearly midnight in Logrono; everything seemed sleeping, save the pale moon and the twinkling stars that sparkled so brightly in the blue vault that arched the Spanish city. Here and there the tall spire of a church reached up towards the Heavens, and now and then the heavy column of a convent chapel lifted itself above the humbler dwellings that nestled about its base. A careful ear would detect, at intervals, the notes of a guitar breaking on the stillness, as some gallant cavalier sang beneath the balcony of his lady-love. But still more quiet grew the streets, and more subdued were the pulsations of the town, until it was past the hour of twelve, when a figure, closely muffled, turned an angle in the wall of the house of Alvarez, leading by the hand what, in the deep shadow of the moon cast on the building, seemed to be a boy. The stealthy movements of the two shewed at once that their business, be it what it might, was of a character that required both caution and secrecy.

The lowest windows on the side of the house where they now were must have been at least ten feet from the ground, and these were secured by iron crossbars well imbedded in the wall itself; while the massive folding doors or gate that formed the only entrance to the court-yard of the house, looked, with its sides covered by big-headed spikes, almost impregnable even to a systematic attack of soldiery. But it soon became evident that it was the object of the parties to obtain an entrance in some way; and there had already been added a third person to their number, who seemed to have been lingering behind, partly to bring up the rear in safety, and partly because he seemed to feel that his presence had not until now become necessary.

"This is the second window from the gate," said she who had directed the lad's steps, and who, now that she had loosened the garments that she had kept so closely wrapped about her, showed herself to be a woman of large stature, and one of that numerous class known as gitanas or gipsys.

As she spoke she deposited an ingeniously formed step or brace ladder which she had brought concealed under her dress, and with a cautionary word to the boy by her side, she mounted this to the top, some four feet, and raising the child after her in her arms, with a strength that would have done credit to a professed mountebank, she placed him upon the sill of the window, and prepared to thrust his slender body through the iron cross bars. The boy remained passive, as if waiting for directions.

"Can you get through?" asked the woman, in a suppressed voice, of the child.

"I think so, with a little squeezing," replied the boy, pushing his head and shoulders through the space between the bars, by way of trial.

"Are the bars too close for you?"

"No."

"You understand the directions, Minnetta?"

"To go down the stairs into the court, and unbar the large doors for you to enter."

"Exactly. Follow along the whole length of the corridor, and when you get down to the court below, come back just the same distance, and you will be opposite us, as we shall be on the outside of the doors. Move lightly, and slip the bolts easy. Rio and I will wait for you."

"I understand," said the boy, with an impatient movement, as though he would be on his errand without further delay.

"Then get in as quickly as possible," said the gipsy, aiding him by a vigorous push from behind, in his struggles to get his body through the small aperture afforded by the iron bars.

As the child disappeared through the window, the gipsy came down, and with her companion placed herself at the gate.

The gipsy race were at the height of their strength and power at the period to which we now refer. Cunning, almost to witchcraft, they seemed to possess means of information and foresight that were almost miraculous. Like all of their tribes, earlier and later, they lived by preying upon the rights of others, and stealing was reduced by them to a science which they carefully taught their children, as the only legacy and inheritance that circumstances permitted them to leave for their future support.

In the use of poisons and remedies, they surpassed the most cunning disciples of Galen; and were not only thoroughly disliked by the better classes, but feared and dreaded by them. At times large numbers of valuable cattle would be taken suddenly ill, and swell up as though they were like to die; when three or four gipsys would make their appearance, and having secretly administered the poison which had produced this effect, they knew the antidote, therefore, which they applied, and having recovered the cattle, they were of course richly rewarded. This was only one of the many tricks and devices practised by the gipsys who lingered about the country towns; but it serves to show their general character.

The three persons whom we have seen lurking about the house of Alvarez, and one of whom had already entered, were of this class, as their dress and language betokened.

Ample time had already elapsed for the boy to have performed the task allotted to him, and the two persons who awaited him at the gate began to show some tokens of impatience.

"Surely this business cannot have miscarried," said the woman, who was evidently the leader in the business. "Have you heard any voices from within, Rio?"

"Once I thought that I did," said the man. "Hist! don't you hear something?"

"Nothing," said the woman. "What is it like?"

"Like voices and hurried steps."

"I hear it now; but stay, we will wait for the last chance, after risking so much to get in."

"Minnetta?" suggested the man, referring to the lad within the house.

"Must be left behind; there is no help for it now," said the woman.

"Let us away," said the man.

"There's no fear of immediate pursuit. But come, we had better get to the camp, for we have stirred up a nest that will bring hornets about our ears unless we are away by daylight."

A moment after several lights were displayed at the windows, and the sound of stern voices from within showed that the house was aroused and prepared for any emergency. This being evident, the gipsys, with hasty but reluctant strides, turned their steps away from the house, and with rapid speed sought the protection of their camp without the city walls.

Leaving the gipsys to make the best of their way out of the city, we will follow Minnetta into the house of Alvarez, to see the result of his unceremonious visit.

Those without, when they had thrust the child through the bars of the window, were very sure that every soul of the household was by that time deep lost in the forgetfulness of sleep ; but as it happened, the lord of the house, Don Francisco, with his secretary, had been engaged until past midnight upon some literary researches, and were just then passing by the main corridor, when, to their no small amazement, the gipsy child was thrust through the bars of the window as already described, and came tumbling most unceremoniously at their feet.

"What have we here?" asked Don Francisco, suddenly starting back and drawing his sword.

"Only a boy, my lord," said the secretary, who had also loosened his dagger.

"'Tis a boy indeed!"

"And unarmed, my lord."

"Yes ; but there must be more behind. Look to that window, while I give the alarm."

"Aye, my lord ;" said the secretary, drawing his dagger and approaching the window, while the gipsy child, having gained its feet, leaned quietly against the wall, as though a glance had shewn it that an attempt to escape, or resistance, were both entirely useless.

The alarm signal being given, it had sent the lights dancing in all directions, for its import was well understood by the entire household. Those lights being displayed at the port windows had been one of the intimations to the child's accomplices that their object was frustrated. It required but a few moments to satisfy the household that, let the attempt which had been discovered be intended for what it might, it had been abandoned, and there was no further cause for fear.

"Your name, my boy?" asked Don Francisco of the strange child who had been led before him to his study for examination, after the bustle and surprise were over.

No answer came from the prisoner, who stood with downcast eyes and a careless mien, swinging a silver whistle that hung from his neck over and over the fingers of the right hand.

"Who are you, and from whence are you come?" continued Don Francisco. "If you answer us well, we have no desire but to see our own property protected."

"My lord, he will not answer your question," said the secretary, much interested.

"Will you not reply to us?" continued Don Francisco. "It were better for your own interest that you should do so, and at once."

But still the child maintained a dogged silence, not even raising his eyes from the floor where they had fallen on his first entering the room.

"In the morning, my lord, perhaps the prisoner will think better of this," suggested the secretary.

After a few more ineffectual attempts to draw any information from the young gipsy, for such they at once discovered the prisoner to be, the lad was appointed a place to sleep in until the morning, while a watch was set with strict precautions as to vigilance, and thus the night wore away. To the child it was a bitter long night—oh, how bitter ! he longed so for the fresh air, for freedom and a chance for breath. To one who had slept from infancy beneath the open sky, or at most sheltered only by a rude tent from the open air, the confinement of stone walls and closed doors was almost insupportable. But the child was overcome with fatigue, and at last even the gipsy slept.

Not so the guard, who had received his orders from his master as to watchfulness. In his humble mind there was operating a superstitious horror at the task that had been imposed upon him. In common with his class generally in Spain, he attributed to the gipsys supernatural powers, and as the child slept, he half expected every moment to see the wall open and the boy carried away in a blaze of light, or something else quite as extraordinary and wonderful.

But the day broke at last, and no miracle had astounded the superstitious guard.

A DISCOVERY.

CHAPTER II.

A faithful but dumb companion—Description of a gipsy youth—The fair Signorita Isadora—Effect of kindness—The faithful hound—A perplexing discovery.

——" I' the name of truth,
Are ye fantastical, or that indeed
Which outwardly ye shew ?"—*Macbeth.*

WHEN the warder who had charge of the gates that opened from the street into the house of Alvarez, opened them on the morning referred to in the close of the last chapter, a fox hound sprang by him, and with his nose to the ground ran hither and thither, as though intent upon discovering some one. The dog was of a remarkably intelligent and sagacious breed, and seemed highly trained; for although running around in the greatest excitement, it uttered not a single cry or howl, until at last it came to the entrance of the room where the gipsy was confined, when it dropped as though it had lost all life, and assuming a watchful attitude, with its eyes upon the entrance, it remained fixed and motionless.

The warden, who had followed the animal in some surprise, was a man who could appreciate instinct and training in a hound, for he had charge of his master's hawks and dogs, and he was not a little pleased at the sight presented by the animal referred to.

"That was finely done," mused the warden to himself; "not a howl, a bark, or even a whine, but as steady and persevering as a human creature—ay, a very gipsy, like its young master. Now I would wager my dagger that no abuse or cunning could elicit a sound from that faithful creature. 'Fore Heaven, but the boy shall have his dog—there can be no harm in that."

As the kind-hearted warden spoke, he opened the door, and the hound, with a single bound, was at the gipsy's side, his nose fondled in the boy's hand, while ever and anon he turned a look with his big round eyes first upon the guard and then on the warden, that told how fierce he could be, when incited to act by a sign from the gipsy. But no thought of this sort seemed to cross the boy's mind. He looked grateful even to the warden who had let his dumb companion in to his presence. On the dog itself the boy seemed to look with a love that was not to be mistaken.

The household of Don Francisco Alvarez was not materially discomposed by the events of the previous night. It was evident that the gipsy had intended to rob the house, seconded by his companions, had chance not discovered and defeated them. But there was no evidence of anger, or an intent to revenge himself, on the part of the master of the house, for the evil attempt that had been made against him, and when the lad who had been introduced into the window was called for examination, Don Francisco looked upon him with a feeling of pity for his youth and guilt, rather than with any feeling of anger. And thus he gazed upon him in silence for some minutes.

The child, for the gipsy was scarcely more than a child, seemed touched by the kind manner which Don Francisco bore towards him, and losing the sulky air of the previous night, he raised his fine dark eyes and bright intellectual face, to give back the glance of kindness and hospitality that were so considerately intended to reassure and calm the feelings of the prisoner.

"Have my people been kind to thee?" asked Don Francisco, in a gentle tone.

"Yes," said the gipsy, stooping to answer the hound, who nestled so close to his side, and whose manner seemed to say, "I'll stick by you, master," and then its fierce eye was bent on the persons of those present, before whom the gipsy had been summoned for examination.

"By what name are you known?" continued the master of the house.

"They call me Minnetta; though I have a dozen names, as occasion may require," replied the gipsy, toying with a heavy tassel that was attached to some drapery on the wall, and seeming much to wonder what the use of such an article could possibly be.

"Where are the tribe to which you belong?"

"Yesterday they were near the city walls, encamped at the spring: but ere this I suppose they are miles away from here."

"Why do you think so?" asked Don Francisco.

"Had the last night's attempt succeeded, they were to have marched with the break of day, and its failure is only an additional reason for an early start," said the boy, carelessly.

Don Francisco mused to himself in silence, and could not but be struck with the intelligence and shrewdness of one so young as the prisoner; besides which, his personal appearance was calculated to challenge no slight degree of interest, and, indeed, a good share of admiration also.

The youth was much better dressed than was the custom with the roving tribes of the times that wandered over the length and breadth of the country. Indeed, the dress must have been stolen from some page's wardrobe, and had evidently been put on for this occasion, as the gipsy seemed at times but ill at ease in it. The limbs were cased in silken hose, that extended above the knees, displaying a limb of full and faultless proportions, and were there met by the full silken drawers, of scarlet and blue, like the more modern Spanish court style. The doublet and jacket were of green velvet, with golden bell-buttons, and trimmed with silver cord and braid, altogether forming a most picturesque and becoming costume.

The wearer graced well this jaunty dress, and, save a slight effeminacy and almost womanly beauty of the face, was very handsome. The expression of the eye was puzzling; it was roguish, and yet half confiding, and though cunning might be read there, yet it seemed rather assumed than natural. During the pause to which we have referred, the boy looked about him with no little curiosity, to see the rich gilding, silken hangings, and carved furniture that adorned the room; and a close observer might have detected a slight curl of contempt in the movement of his handsome lips, as he regarded these useless trappings and ornaments. The uses of nearly all the luxuries that met the gipsy's eyes were to him a mystery.

By the side of Don Francisco Alvarez, stood a young and pretty creature, a fair signorita, who was watching the gipsy's face and manner with more than usual interest, while he gazed thus about the room, and the secretary mended his pen to record the intended examination. Isadora, Don Francisco's child, was one of those delicate, but finely-formed figures, that are so often found among the high-born Castilians, with features of faultless regularity and beauty; and even the gipsy had been gazing at her with no slight tokens of admiration since his entrance into the apartment.

But a new feature was now given to affairs by Don Francisco resuming the examination.

"For what purpose did you enter my house last night?" continued the master.

"To rob you!" answered the gipsy, without one moment of hesitation.

"Indeed? you are very frank," said Don Francisco, not a little surprised at the answer.

"You asked me, and I have told you the truth," said the prisoner, calmly.

"I believe that you have," answered Don Francisco; "but I had feared that you would attempt to deceive me."

"No, signor," said the gipsy; "from a child I have been taught to steal, but not to lie."

"This is a strange sort of morality," said Don Francisco. "But was robbery your only purpose?"

"I think our people had some other design, but what it was I know not. My part was to open the door."

"Most frankly answered," said Don Francisco, to his secretary.

After asking a few more questions of a like import, the examination was, for the present, discontinued, but the secretary still continued to regard the gipsy with the utmost earnestness. There was a pride and defiance in the expression of the prisoner's eye that challenged admiration in one so young, and there was also a quiet assumption of dignity, that showed the gipsy must hold more than ordinary rank and respect among those with whom he associated. Not more than fifteen years could have passed over that young form, but those years had been passed in exposure to the elements, and beneath the ripening influence of sunshine and the open air. It was thus that the nut-brown of the cheek was so soft and olive in its hue, and it was this roving and exposed life that had made that young form so elastic—so straight and graceful in its naturalness.

These graces and beauties in the gipsy prisoner filled Isadora's eyes, the young daughter of the lord of Alvarez, and both she and the secretary regarded him with increasing interest. Even the hound that kept so close to its master's side seemed to share in the intense observation that the gipsy elicited, and none there could help marking its earnest and steady devotion, and the dumb show of affection that actuated it. It was now crouching upon the floor, regardless of all around, and looking steadily into its young master's eyes.

"I cannot yet release you," said Don Francisco to his prisoner, "and you must content yourself to remain here with me for the present. I would not confine you," he continued; "it is against my will; but yet I can hardly trust you, lest you should seize upon the first opportunity to start away."

This was said in a tone half interrogatory, in order to try the gipsy; but it elicited no reply, and the young prisoner remained with downcast eyes, while a half-stubborn expression crept over the face. The gipsy even turned half away, and resumed the tassel that had been once before in his hands; but it was plain enough that strong emotions were working within, beneath his assumed in-difference.

Don Francisco marked well the bearing of his prisoner. He knew the spirit that ever actuates the gipsy—he knew how doubly bitter confinement of any sort was to him, born as he was, in the open air, and acknow-ledging no master, and knowing no roof save the broad arch of Heaven itself. He realized all this, but yet he felt that there was no security but confinement for the boy; and sending for his steward, he ordered a chain upon the gipsy's ankle, and the prisoner to be locked up for safe keeping.

It was not until the shackle and chain were brought, and even fastened about the limb, that the gipsy's raised eyes met those of Isadora, when a sort of appeal seemed to beam from them for a single moment. The effect was electrical; for the fair signorita dropped upon her knee beside her father, and begged him to order the chain removed, saying that she would herself answer for the prisoner's good faith and security. The cavalier looked for a moment from one to the other, and said :

"'Tis but poor security you offer me."

"He will not attempt to escape if you treat him kindly, father," said Isadora.

"For thy sake, my child, it shall be so. Remove the shackle," he continued, to the steward.

The gipsy's breast heaved quickly as the order was given for the removal of the chain. It was the first token of real emotion that he had evinced. When Don Francisco said :

"May I trust you that you will not leave these walls without my consent ?"

"You may," said the gipsy; "though the open fields are very dear to me."

"I am satisfied," said Don Francisco; "let the gipsy be treated as our guest."

This disposition of matters not a little sur-prised the household, who had assembled to witness some exemplary punishment bestowed upon one of the hated and persecuted race. And now for the first time the gipsy loosed the hound, who, the moment that the chain was brought towards his master, had shown a silent but fixed and bloody purpose on any one that touched him. It was the gipsy's own careful endeavors that had prevented the hound from springing at once upon the steward.

All restraint being now removed, Isadora called the gipsy aside, and was soon deeply engaged in asking a thousand questions of the roving life that his people led ; for though the general characteristics of the race were familiar to her, yet they were rarely found in a condition to afford any personal information relating to themselves, and in-deed rarely were willing to do so to any one. But Isadora had acted as a sort of deliverer for the prisoner; and a keen sense of gratitude on the gipsy's part led to a very free and agreeable chat between them touching the subject referred to.

On the subsequent day, Isadora came to her father, with her face depicting an odd medley of expressions, and Don Francisco was curious to know what could so have excited his child.

"Father, you will not be angry with our prisoner if I tell you of a deception that has been practised upon you, will you ?" com-menced Isadora, earnestly.

"What's the matter now, eh? has the rogue forgotten his promise and decamped ?"

"No, father, not that," said Isadora, still hesitating to explain herself.

"Well, what is it, then? speak out, my child ; you have no cause for fear, surely."

"Why, our gipsy prisoner, father, is a—a—'

"What, Isadora ?"

"A *girl*, father, that's all !" said Isadora, blushing as though she were to blame.

CHAPTER III.

The wild bird's wings are clipped—Astonishment of a gipsy at civilized luxuries—The Spanish Gipsy's skill in horsemanship—A real virago —The gipsy trick—The belle of Logrono.

"The courser pawed the ground with restless feet,
And snorting, foamed, and champed the golden bit."
DRYDEN.

THE wonder attendant upon the dis-covery which Isadora had announced to her father, touching the sex of the new comer, created not a little surprise at first, and filled the retainers of the house with amazement. He who had acted as guard over the prisoner on the first night, now declared that he saw nothing surprising in all this, for a gipsy had power to do one miracle as well as another; and, indeed, to give still more effect and importance to his opinion, he boldly hinted at some super-natural demonstrations which had manifested themselves during the first night's watch. The subject ceased at once to be matter of remark in the family, and dropped into the hands of the menials of the house, who would not at once give up such a capital subject for gossip.

Isadora Alvarez and the gipsy girl Minnetta, being of just about the same age and size, it was a very easy matter to supply the new comer with every article of dress appropriate to her sex and the company in which she now found herself. Isadora's wardrobe was freely opened to her, and Minnetta seemed never tired of examining and trying on every article that presented itself to her curious eyes. Her high-bred companion could not but acknowledge the remarkable beauty of her protégé, whose fine dark olive complexion, the bronzed hue of the skin, and whose dark, piercing eyes, beaming forth from features of faultless regularity and beauty, altogether formed a charming and delightful picture.

What a new field opened itself to the study and contemplation of the gipsy daughter! How novel and strange was everything that met her gaze! The luxury of every appointment was a theme of amazement, and could be compared to nothing that she had ever seen or heard of. The regular and sumptuous meals, and the utensils used at the table, puzzled her. The distinction between master and servant, so rigidly observed, and the lines so carefully drawn, were also the subject of anxious consideration. Everything was strange—everything was new. At first she did not know whether to be pleased or not; struggling in her heart between her natural womanly feelings and the sterner principles that had been taught her in gipsy life, of contempt for all needless and comparatively useless articles. The woman prevailed in her heart, and Minnetta was delighted.

Of course Don Francisco took measures, through the authorities, to institute a search for the gipsy depredators, and pursuing them closely. The soldiery had very nearly come to a contest with them; but the band at last made good their escape in the wilds of the distant sierra. After satisfying himself that there would be no further attempt upon his house, still, under the circumstances, Don Francisco felt fully authorized to retain in partial confinement one who had been taken upon his grounds under such suspicious appearances. Indeed, Minnetta had grown to be an immense favorite with all the household, save one, as will eventually appear, so that none would willingly have now parted from her. Her extraordinary aptness to learn, and yet her extreme simplicity and innocence, were constant themes of interest to Isadora and her father.

"Well, Minnetta," said Don Francisco, one day, "it is time that I should tell you, that you are no longer a prisoner here, but are free to come and go at your own pleasure."

"Am I to go?" said the gipsy girl, startled at the idea, and a tear filling her eye in a moment.

"Are you willing, then, to remain with us?" asked the cavalier, observing her closely.

"Willing! Ah, where else should I go now?" said the gipsy girl, with downcast eyes.

"True," said Don Francisco; "come hither, Minnetta." And taking her hand, and drawing her to his side, the cavalier told her that she should be Isadora's sister, and always welcome to his board.

"I cannot bear to think that I trespass upon you; but since you have taught me so much, and to live so differently, I feel that I am much changed, and hardly fit again to seek the tents of our people upon the mountain side or the open moor."

"Speak not of it, Minnetta; let this be your home for the future, and be as happy as you can."

The gipsy girl could make no reply, but she turned away with a swelling heart and heaving breast. She had indeed been changed, greatly changed, by the events of the last few weeks; and she fully realised this. Leaving Don Francisco, she sought her own apartment, and reviewed her present situation with contending emotions, and feeling that in her change of life—though it had been brought about by such a questionable agency—she had been fortunately thrown among those who had already proved themselves the best of friends to her.

Notwithstanding these feelings and demonstrations on her part, still Minnetta did secretly pine now and then, even to tears, for the open air, the freedom and unconstraint of the gipsy life. Its fascinations, in spite of all the comforts and advantages by which she was surrounded, almost proverbial for its intensity, was strong upon her heart; and the poor girl found it hard, very hard, to break herself of those long familiar habits which had become necessary to her comfort, if not to her life itself. Thus it was that for months after she had found a home at Don Francisco's, she was often found sleeping at midnight beneath the stars in the open court upon the ground, with only her blanket wrapped around her, and a rude billet of wood for a pillow, while her faithful hound nestled by her side, wakeful at her slightest movement, and growling defiance at the approach of any one.

Often when Don Francisco and his daughter rode outside the city walls, accompanied by their train of servants and men-at-arms, Minnetta was invited to go with them; and choosing on such occasions the most spirited courser in all the stud, she rode him with a free rein and a fearless air, that made even the best horsemen among the retainers of the house of Alvarez to envy her.

It was mere sport for her to tame the haughty mettle of the animal, and to sit him with the ease and assurance of a professed equestrian. There was no timidity, no yielding; but it was the steady hand and fixed purpose of the rider that brought submission. From childhood she had done thus—aye, often with a simple rope for a bit, and perhaps even no saddle at all. Her gipsy life had taught her to mount and direct the proudest Andalusian horses, that came of a stock as old and as proud as that of the princes of the land themselves. This had been Minnetta's school.

The followers of Don Francisco would sometimes detect a flush of secret admiration shooting across her brow, as he observed these feats of horsemanship; and though he rarely spoke of them, yet there seemed some secret power of appreciation that strongly affected him. The cavalier himself was considered an extraordinary horseman; and none knew where he had learned to carry so free a rein and so light a stirrup; albeit there were some vague hints of his once having lived over the sea, among the Moors, who ride their horses as though they were part of the animal.

Though Minnetta sometimes felt the loss of her freedom, still it is surprising how quickly the body and the mind will accommodate themselves to the luxuries of life, though both may have been strangers to them before. Thus it was with the gipsy daughter. Those things that at first had only called forth her disdain, as being unworthy the use of a free and healthful body, were now shared with Isadora, and even the studies that had been proposed to her, grew day by day to interest her more as she saw her more highly cultivated friend improving them; and finally she really commenced to master this lesson and that, as given and explained to them by the good old Dominican father, the friar of St. Levitico, attached to the house of Alvarez.

The only drawback to the pleasure and enjoyment of the two young girls was that of the prying interference and constant annoyance of the Signora Alvarez, Don Francisco's second wife; the first having survived the birth of their daughter but a few months. The present lady of the house was one of that class whose temper seems to have been so completely soured as to turn to acid everything with which it comes in contact. Her only joy appeared to be in planning trouble for others; and she was only comparatively happy in contemplating the misery she had caused to operate upon Isadora, Minnetta, or possibly Don Francisco himself, whom she by no means spared, though he heeded her but slightly. We say, save the machinations of this vile-spirited woman, the two girls had nothing to annoy them.

"Now if mother would only cease to annoy us so," said Isadora, good-naturedly, "how very happy and comfortable we should be, Minnetta, wouldn't we?"

"Yes, I am sure of that, Isadora, for I begin to feel quite happy already, in spite of her unkindness," said the gipsy girl honestly, in reply.

"It does seem as if she might let us alone, for we never trouble her," said Isadora, pettishly.

"Oh yes; we do."

"Why, how, Minnetta?"

"By being happy, Isadora. But I should like to give her a gipsy punishment; such an one as she would remember for a time at least."

"What is that?"

"Duck her, to be sure. Half drown her, and make her bless her stars that she wasn't drowned altogether. It's a capital cure for crabbedness. I've seen it tried many a time."

"That would be almost too severe, though I can't say I have much love for her."

At that moment Signora Alvarez, who had been listening to the young girls, rushed into the room, actuated by a passion that seemed to defy all control. Poor Isadora trembled like a leaflet in the wind, but the gipsy girl knew no fear. She had been educated to fear nothing, and therefore drawing herself up in a calm and dignified manner, she awaited the storm that she felt was about to burst upon her. It came at last, and the signora raved, until losing her temper altogether, she rushed upon Minnetta, with uplifted hand, to strike her. She was a large and well-built woman, of some forty years of age, and her blow would have been no child's play.

Minnetta did not stir, but contracting her own hand with the knuckles upward, she received the signora's blow, her knuckles striking upon her wrist. The gipsy girl's hand was stationary, so that in reality it was her angry antagonist who struck herself; and so acute was the pain caused by the gipsy trick, that Isadora's step-mother retired, crying aloud—

"Oh how unfortunate that this should have occurred," said Isadora.

"True; but I could not permit her to strike me, and I was resolved to teach her a lesson which would prevent a recurrence of such an attempt."

But if Signora Alvarez was unkind to her step-daughter and the young gipsy, Don Francisco more than counterbalanced it by his own unvarying kindness to them both. No enticement could probably have caused the gipsy to leave him now, though no argument or course of treatment had been adopted to induce her to give up her former mode of life, other than the argument of example and constant kind treatment from her protector and companion, Isadora.

In the meantime, Minnetta, shewing a natural tact and shrewdness that enabled her to surmount every opposing obstacle that presented itself, fitted herself hourly for the proud circles that her intercourse with her patron's friends constantly brought her in contact with. Her story being generally known in Logrono, any little outré remarks or exhibition of feeling on her part were received with all due allowance for her early associations and want of polite experience.

But the truth was, her own natural good taste, and her air of naïveté, crowned all she said and did with a charm.

"Now, Minnetta, if I had said such a thing as that, the whole circle would have laughed at me for it; but coming from you, they repeat the remark as a capital thing. I declare it is too bad to be so completely eclipsed as I am." Isadora said this with an arch smile and pretended feeling.

"Take care, Isadora," replied the gipsy girl, kissing her cheek; "have a care, or if you talk so I shall think that you, if no one else, make fun of me."

For months the gipsy girl led this sort of life, until she became a belle. Her remarkable maturity of form, owing to her early life, and her free, off-hand, though not unpolished manner, might have led to the idea of her being much older than she really was, and indeed she did seem so; and thus, when she was on the verge of sixteen, the young cavaliers were all ready to couch a lance for her, or almost to worship at her feet, so perfect and beautiful had she grown in her womanly charms.

The gipsy child was not, however, always so free and thoughtless as she seemed; there were memories that lingered in her heart of the open heath. But we will not anticipate.

CHAPTER IV.

The fair daughter of Don Francisco—The bitterness of envy—A quaint old room full of strange things—A strange pantomime by moonlight—The discovery and surprise—Force of habit.

"How use doth breed a habit in a man."—SHAKSPERE.

IN placing our characters properly before the mind's eye of the reader, we should not for a moment forget to present Don Francisco's fair daughter in her true light.

Isadora was less beautiful than her singular companion, but yet possessed an ever-charming and gentle grace, though by no means lacking the true pride of her rank. Her features, abstractedly considered, were far from being homely; and then the real delight she seemed to take in shewing Minnetta's good qualities and brilliant characteristics, seemed to enhance and beautify her own. Nor was Isadora without her admirers. Indeed, the house of Alvarez had become the resort of half the gallant young cavaliers of the city, much to the annoyance of the ugly signora, who sought still, in a hundred different ways, to torment and vex not only the girls themselves, but their noble visitors.

It is astonishing how active an agent envy will soon become in the human heart. Here was a noble Spanish lady completely under its control, resorting to the most petty acts of meanness to gratify the envy that filled her heart. Signora Alvarez was the victim of circumstances. Had she been married at a more congenial period of her life, and had Heaven seen fit to give her children to *love*, perhaps that spirit, in room of the bitter one that now tenanted her heart, would have blessed her. At least, let us, in charity to her feelings, believe that this would have been the case.

Among the rear offices of the house of Alvarez, in that portion of the long and broad corridor that surrounded the courtyard below, and at the farthest part from the rooms appointed for domestic uses, was a large storage apartment, filled with lumber and old rubbish, the accumulation of years gone by. Here and there upon the floor lay a broken sword, or a battered helmet, with old rusty armour, and long blunted spears, that had been used on the fields of Arragon centuries before.

Here again lay moth-eaten silken doublets, and rusty coats of mail: and beside them, the caparisons of a horse accoutred for the tournament. On the wall in the dim light were hanging tattered banners, and the armorial bearings of the house, in various styles. It was a quaint old lot of stuff that filled the room, so suggestive of the past, and teaching such a lesson of humble pride and decay. For those who had once filled those silken garments, or fought in those coats of mail, though fired in their day by ambition, and prompted by pride, were now outlived by those very trappings they had worn, themselves forgotten even in name:

"Their sceptres broken, and their swords in rest."

There was an occurrence relating to this ancient store-room that has a bearing upon our story, which occurred at this time ; and to Don Francisco and his daughter, it was one of no slight interest.

They were walking together in the spacious corridor already described, conversing, and now and then pausing to look upwards at the wonderful brightness of the star-lit heavens. The moon was at its full, the atmosphere clear, and they seemed almost to feel the wonderful light that poured down upon them in the still evening hour. It seemed to hallow their very feelings, and Isadora clung more closely to her father's arm, while the proud cavalier looked down upon her with infinite tenderness, and pressed his lips to her fair brow with a whispered blessing.

"It is just such a night, my child, as I have watched so many times in far off Morocco, among those hard task-masters, the wild Moors," said her father, thoughtfully.

"Father, you have never told me how it was that you were a prisoner among that strange people," said Isadora, looking up lovingly into his face.

"Nor can I do so now, my child. At some future time I will speak to thee of this ; enough that I tasted the bitter pill of slavery among those Moorish infidels."

"But you will tell me some time, father, won't you ?" asked Isadora, so tenderly and beseechingly, that her father pressed her still closer to his side, as he answered—

"Yes ; the time will probably come when all will be known ; but there are scenes in the past, my child, relating to thy father's history, that he would gladly forget—aye, that he would efface, if it were in his power, at almost any cost."

"What was that singular noise ?" asked Isadora, as she started and turned towards the store-room—a place that was seldom or ever intruded upon by any one.

"Hark ! I did hear something within there," said Don Francisco, as both drew towards the broad and lofty window that opened from the apartment upon the corridor where they stood.

"There it is again !" said Isadora. "How very odd it is."

They both now approached the window, and gazed curiously into the moon-lit, but dreary-looking room. The light entered from both sides, the battlement window admitting it from the outer wall, and from the window that opened into the centre of the house— the building being in the Moorish style of a hollow square—the moon struck in full rays upon the glistening steel and weapon points, and lay along the dusty floor in a flood of light. Amid all this, they discovered a figure wrapped in the tattered habiliments of a gitana, one of the roving bands of the country. The figure wore a female dress, and moved with stealthy strides among the old armour and cast-off battle-gear that filled the room.

"How came she here, father, and what does she want ?" asked Isadora, in a whisper.

"Hist ! my child," said the father, holding up his finger to enforce the injunction.

Though as much amazed as his child could be at seeing such a creature within his walls, Don Francisco said nothing, but with Isadora almost held his breath, to observe undiscovered the singular movements of the woman. The light was too dim to discover her countenance, but all of her movements were perfectly distinct, and these were of such a strange character as to completely puzzle them.

Now the figure sat down upon the floor, and seemed by her movements to be joining in a repast with invisible spirits, breaking imaginary bread and eating with them ; and now, rising with outstretched arms, she seemed to be dancing with a company like herself, in a circle round and round the spot where they had been eating just before. This was repeated several times, and then the scene changed, and the active, agile form was bent as if by age, the clothes gathered closely around the head as if to avoid

EFFECT OF MUSIC ON THE GIPSIES.

observation and screen the face, and then seizing a staff, she tottered up to this spot and to that, with bended head and humble air, as if she were begging. Now she stopped before a hanging suit of armour, and by gesticulations, begged most piteously; and now sinking down half dead with seeming fatigue, she pleaded in dumb show before some antique piece of furniture, as though it had been some rich old cavalier or signora.

But these movements were soon changed. The air of suppliance was dropped: the seeming decrepitude gave place to a sprightly and cat-like movement—the clothes were thrown off the face, a sharp dagger was loosened at the belt, and its point even was felt, and then the strange figure stole here and there among the rubbish as stealthily and warily as a thief, while Don Francisco and Isadora gazed at her still with undisguised amazement at these unaccountable actions; and then at last, after these movements were completed, the figure wrapped itself in its robes of tattered cloth, and throwing itself upon the hard floor, seemed for a time to sleep; but this, like other portions of the pantomime, was only for a minute in duration, when the figure again changed its position.

"This is very, very strange, father," said Isadora, drawing a long breath. "This woman must surely be mad;" and as she spoke, she clung more closely to her father's arm.

"Fear not, my child," said Don Francisco, thoughtfully, "there is no cause for alarm;" and still he regarded the strange scene within the room with an interest that was most intense.

Isadora felt almost affrighted to see her father so deeply impressed. He seemed to be unable to remove his eyes from the figure and her movements, and his daughter felt a mysterious dread creeping over her every moment that now passed. She no longer looked within the room, but at her father, whose eyes were still fixed there with the same extraordinary interest.

"See! she is coming this way, father," said Isadora, who had turned once more to look at the figure. At the same time she drew her father back, while the figure that they had been thus minutely watching, turned its steps towards the corridor where they had stood.

"Stand aside, Isadora, quietly; we will see what her purpose may be before we interrupt her," said Don Francisco, drawing his daughter to one side, where they were partially screened, while the figure came out of the room, and after throwing a furtive glance about her, hurried at once towards the apartments appropriated to the domestic uses of the family.

"Stay here, my child," said Isadora's father.

A sudden thought seemed to come over Don Francisco, as he left his daughter's side, and springing quickly forward to that of the strange figure, he arrested her progress by forcibly laying his hand upon her arm. The figure turned suddenly, and confronted him with a slight exclamation of surprise.

"I thought so," said Don Francisco, more to himself than to her before him.

It was Minnetta, the Spanish gipsy!

In a moment more, Don Francisco turned away from her without saying a word; and, taking Isadora's arm, led her, by another entrance, into the drawing-room of the house. He seemed at once, by some singular instinct, to fathom the entire mystery of this odd behaviour, and to require no explanation.

"Where is that woman gone, father?" asked Isadora, as soon as they had reached the room.

"It matters not, my child; never refer to what you have seen to-night to any one." While he spoke, he buried his face in his hands, and seemed to lose himself in secret thoughts.

Isadora knew her father's moods. Indeed he was not unfrequently thus; and so kissing him tenderly, she bade him good night, and sought her own room, not a little puzzled.

Few persons can realize the force of habit: it was very strong at times upon the fair young gipsy. From childhood she had been instructed in the wiles of this roving people, and she had, with growing years practised their arts and cunning, until the exercise of these qualities had become almost a second nature to her. She could not help at times longing for the open fields and the rude tents of her early home; and at these times she pined like a caged bird, for those habits which had inured her to exposure and hardship, redering both almost pleasurable to her.

At times these feelings would come over her so strongly, as to amount almost to a monomania, and she would imagine herself once more a gipsy girl in the camp, and at the rude meal of a gitana. Once more only the broad sky was over her, and the winds of Heaven fanned her cheek. It was while under the powerful influence of one of these fits of memory that she had sought, not for the first time, the old store-room, where she imagined herself living over the past, and personating the part that she had so often enacted in reality when a wandering gipsy.

It was, as she had told Don Francisco, a fact, that the lessons which had been taught her were so potent as to make her resolve never again to join voluntarily the gipsy league; but these periodical turns of feeling were beyond her control, and she gave way to them. If at that very moment those who had led her thither had appeared, and offered to conduct her back again to the tents of her people, she would have bidden them go without her. She saw now with different eyes. She could never again act upon those principles that had been taught her in her childhood—they were banished from her heart now.

When she found that Don Francisco had thus discovered her, Minnetta realized that she must have been overlooked, and hasten-ing to her room, she wept, half in mortification, and half, perhaps, in vexation, that she should have been found indulging in the propensities of her gipsy life. But she was not one to mourn long over anything, and so tossing loose the rich heavy abundance of black hair that covered her head, and laying aside the gear that she had just been enshrouded in, she lay down to sleep, and in a short half hour her gentle respiration and happy face shewed how sweetly she was resting.

Having thus introduced the reader to our principal characters, and portrayed scenes calculated to shew him their exact position, we must now ask him to follow us to more vivid portions of our story.

CHAPTER V.

The student of Salamanca—A wanderer and an outcast—The power of music over the turbid spirit—Dangerous company for a homeless youth—A gipsy beauty and a bride—The student turned gitano.

"There are crimes,
Made venial by the occasion, and temptation,
Which nature cannot master or forbear."—BYRON.

IN order to place the thread of our story so before the reader, that we shall regard the various characters who constitute the *dramatis personæ* with due interest, we must, for a time, change the scene, and carry him to the university of Salamanca, where the youth of the province of Arragon and its vicinity were placed to acquire that which in those days was denominated a finished education.

There wandered forth from the gates of the institution, one calm summer's afternoon, a young and handsome student. His physical appearance would have struck even the casual observer with pleasure, his broad shoulders and finely-developed chest indicating great strength, his firm step, quick, thoughtful eye, and steady compressed lip, denoting spirit and firmness, while his easy and manly grace shewed that his life had been passed with the gentle and refined. He wore the cap and doublet of the university, and looked the scholar and student in his whole appearance. Some sad spirit seemed to actuate him now, for his eye rested upon the ground, and now and then his breast was moved by a heavy sigh. He appeared to be struggling with inward disappointment and crowding thoughts, and at last said, half aloud—

"Well, well, there's no help for it; I might have anticipated this; so the old gentleman discards me altogether. Of course I can't go home, nor be seen in the old-accustomed places. For the present I must be a wanderer. Shall I beg? No, not so bad as that, though my purse is empty, and my wardrobe of the scantiest. I can manage this with some skill," continued he, touching the guitar that was slung to his back, "and discoursing thy sweet notes, my tuneful friend, we will plod on together wherever fortune may lead. With my health and spirits, shall I despair? No, no— the world is wide, I have nothing to lose, and may by chance prove a winner."

Thus musing, the student tugged leisurely along, humming a light serenade as he went. It seemed very evident, by his own words and the apparent circumstances, that he had been guilty of some misdemeanor, of such a character as to banish him from his father's halls; and as his term had closed at the institution, he was like one cast upon the wide world, alone and friendless; but his spirits did not fail him, as we have seen. He bore up bravely against the ill fortune that beset him, and still humming a light Spanish air, he strolled away, unheeding the road he took, and careless whither he went.

Long and weary was the route the student trod; but day by day he beguiled the time with his guitar and the accompaniment of his rich musical voice, and ample and generous was the hospitality that these fine accomplishments won for him at the various stopping-places that fatigue and hunger rendered necessary by the way. Many were the curious adventures that he encountered, sometimes of danger, sometimes of romance, and sometimes of love—themes most congenial to one of his age and temperament—and he was inclined to think at times that his lot was not so *very* hard ; though there were times when he suffered physically, unused as he was to the self-denial that was now unavoidable.

At last, after wandering over half of Spain, now enjoying hospitality and plenty, and now sleeping in the open air, with a stone for a pillow on the mountain side, without the means of allaying the gnawings of hunger, he found himself one afternoon, when on the road from Toledo to Andalusia, over the wild mountains that intersect the route, suddenly surrounded by a band of gitanos. Resistance would have been useless. Though the student lacked not courage, and remained undaunted, yet they were strong in numbers, while he was alone, and carried only his dagger—a weapon no Spaniard was without.

"Hold !" said he, who seemed to lead the rest, "and if you have weapons lay them down at once."

"As to weapons," said the student, quite unmoved, "I have only my dagger, and that you shall fight for, if you must have it." As he said this he unsheathed the blade, which was of the best Damascus.

"You are our prisoner," said the leader of the band, as they drew closer about him ; "what can you offer for your ransom ? Have you gold to give, or shall we toss you from the peak of the cliff, at the rising of to-morrow's sun ? It's a famous height, and those who tempt it make a quick grave."

"Alas !" said the student, without evincing any tokens of fear at the threat he had heard, "I have no gold, no friends, and possess only this guitar—it is my all. Shall I play to you, good gitanos ?"

The gipsies, rather surprised at such a proposition, looked at each other, and then at their prisoner. They were pleased at the calm self-possession that he evinced ; their spirited and hardy natures could appreciate this quality. So, after a few moments pause and consultation among themselves, they lay down upon the greensward in a circle about their prisoner, forming a wild, picturesque group that would have filled a painter's eye. Thus placed, the leader bade him strike his instrument.

The student was of too brave a metal to feel one pang of fear, but still he was fully alive to the peculiarities of his position. He felt that he was playing for his life, and he threw all of his skill and feeling into the touch, and all the power of his voice into the song he sang, pouring forth its rich and culti-vated notes, until those wild rovers, men and women, who surrounded him, stole nearer and nearer to his side, and seemed to watch him with a strange fascination, swaying their bodies back and forth as they sat, or creeping to his very feet, and laying their heads close upon the ground, in the most profound delight. It was a gipsy song he had chosen, one that he had been taught by one of these people, of a much better order of mind than his fellows, and the student had arranged it to his own taste, adding words, and now, in the fervor of the moment, he improvised an illustration of the very scene about him. His effort was completely successful ; he saw and realized his power over the wild spirits around, and each swelling note was the more charming, the more powerful, because of the inspiration of complete success.

He paused, and the stillness, of night reigned about him. Music had saved the student's life, and these wild people, who robbed and murdered all who crossed their path in the mountains, were—

"Tamed and led by this enchantress still."

Indeed from a prisoner the student was raised to the honored privileges of a guest, and bidden to share of the best that their rude hospitality could afford. He was half famished, and partook of the coarse viands set before him by the band, with a zest, and in a manner well calculated to please his captors.

"That man should have been born a gitano," said the leader of the band to one of his followers. "Marked you the fire of his eye, and the calm, unspoken defiance of his purpose ?"

"He showed no fear at our challenge," answered the other, "and looks like one who could act when occasion might require it. As you say, he should have been born one of us."

"We will not part with him easily, he is poor, friendless and a wanderer ; perhaps he may be of service to us with his qualifications. Time will show. Let the people treat him well."

"Aye, that they will do of their own accord," answered the other ; "for they have taken to him already, and see how easily he throws himself upon the ground among them."

"'Tis well," said the leader, turning away thoughtfully, and entering his rude tent, while some of the youngest of the tribe, of both sexes, were dancing to the notes of the tambourine, before the student.

This was dangerous company for the young student to fall into, as the sequel will prove.

He was homeless, almost outlawed, at least so far as his own family and friends were concerned, and as destitute as could well be conceived. He had little to awaken conscience or pride within his breast, and he had wandered thus until he felt quite alone in the world. The gipsies saw in him a stout heart, a ready hand, and, perhaps, withal a desperate spirit; for with their accustomed acuteness, they half read his story at once, while the shrewder ones among them talked of adopting him, and of making their prisoner, the wandering student, by admission into their band, a gitano. They had found a fitting tool for their purpose; for in his present frame of mind he was listless and undecided as to the future, while want and physical suffering will not unfrequently blind all principle and conscience in a man.

It was soon apparent, from the course adopted by the leading persons belonging to the band, that they had resolved, if possible, to bind the student to the gipsy league, and to avail themselves of the qualities which had challenged their admiration in their prisoner, and which, in fact, particularly fitted him for their purpose.

This they could not have so easily accomplished, but for the influence that the daughter of the leader of the band had gained over him by means of her great personal beauty. She was a tall, robust girl, of nearly twenty, but of a beautiful form and natural grace of person, that more than compensated for her robustness of figure. This girl, skilled in all the arts of the gipsy life, cunning, wary, bold in danger, and fearing nothing, was at once captivated by the accomplishments of the student, which seemed to her, in her ignorance of them, to be almost superhuman in their character. Thus the gipsy girl felt that she loved him at once, and was, of course, induced to do all in her power to elicit from him a return of this affection.

Isolated from the world, as it were, and feeling that his position was, in no small degree antagonistical to it, and being bound by a fearful oath not to leave the band until he was formally permitted to do so, the student was, of course, thrown much into the society of Myram, as she was called by the band, and under such circumstances that her beauty and evident desire to please him were not without their effect. There was no cultivation of mind, or beauty of intellect, to captivate him; she was sadly deficient in these respects; but her extraordinary personal attractions, the wild and romantic character of her life, the singular blending of bravery and delicate feelings, that seem to be innate in the human heart, conquered him at last, and he too loved.

The count of the band—as the leader was always called—was of course pleased to see this, for it accorded with his own wishes, and he gave his hearty consent to the marriage of his daughter with the student.

"None but a gitano can marry a gitano," said the count, after giving his assent.

"Am I not one of you?" asked the student, frankly; "bound even by my oath?"

"In part you are one of us; but still you have not yet been formally initiated to our brotherhood."

"True, I have not," said the student; "but what would you have of me?"

"That you should join us in the true gipsy league before you marry Myram."

"I am ready to join you in any way," said the student, after a few moments of thoughtful communing with himself, as though he slightly hesitated before taking the last binding step.

"'Tis well," said the count; "and I will at once see to the arrangements for the ceremony."

"The sooner the better," said the student.

"Then to-night, when the moon hath reached the zenith, the ceremony shall be performed," said the leader, turning from him, with a poorly suppressed gleam of satisfaction depicted on his face.

The student stood where the gipsy had left him for many minutes. He seemed to fully realize that his fate had cast his life for the future among this outlawed race. Some earnest memories of his home and early associations crept over him; a thought, too, of his ambitious labors at the institution of Salamanca, and many such ideas flashed across his brain, and he saw at a glance that he was sacrificing all. It was not without a shudder, and a countenance overshadowed with gloom, that he turned from these musings, and wending his way into the rude camp, sought the gipsy girl's side, to forget in her smiles his heaviness of spirit.

That night was the student inaugurated, with many strange and horrid rites, into the gipsy league, and by oaths and promises that made him tremble for his very soul, should he ever prove false to the interests of the band, or that of any other roving tribe of gipsies in all the broad kingdom of Spain.

The ceremony by which he was made a member of the band was so fearful and disgusting, that he did not recover from the feelings that it produced for many days; but at last, in the dangers and activity of his new life he forgot these things, or grew hardened to them, and found himself as heedless and thoughtless as the rest.   Seeking still for forgetfulness in activity, he astonished the band by his assiduity and earnestness, and no gipsy of the troop could lay claim to the efficacy that their new member evinced in his calling.

Operated upon by a strange fascination re-garding the life which he had adopted, and which a state so nearly approaching to nature seems always to produce, the student soon came to regard the open fields and the blue sky with a true gipsy love, and he slept beneath the blue canopy of Heaven sounder than he had ever done upon a bed of down.

CHAPTER VI.

Conflict with the government troops—Banditti upon the mountain road—The encounter—The victory—A strange scene of carnage—A mystery solved—The gipsy's threat.

"What well-appointed leader fronts us here."—*Henry VI.*

IN the singular manner that we have described, the student was captured by the tribe of gitanos, and being first reconciled, was then made a member of the band.   A short month only had intervened since he first struck his guitar among them, and now he was himself a gipsy.

With his natural intelligence, added to his knowledge of language, ancient and modern, the student acquired, with surprising rapidity, the gitano tongue, a language entirely their own, differing from that of any other people on the face of the globe, though approaching nearest to the Arabic.   Having mastered their language, he was placed by the count as his right-hand man, and being given especial command in time of danger, he grew to be of the utmost service to the troop, and his authority was most cheerfully acknowledged by every member that belonged to the band.

The depredations and audacity of the gipsies upon the highway often led to the calling out of the regular troops, if not to suppress and destroy, at least to intimidate them; but the gipsies grew to be bolder and bolder, not hesitating to attack armed parties even, if not too strong in numbers for them, until, on one of these occasions, when the troops had been called out, and were in hot pursuit of the gipsies, the latter, led on by their count, boldly turned and gave them battle.   The old count was a colossal figure, and a brave and strong man.   He fought like a tiger, slaying a score of troopers, but at last he felt himself pierced by a dozen spear points.   This, of course, decided the day, and the gipsies at once retreated to spots inaccessible to the regular troops, who moved in bodies together, and thus they effected their escape from the king's soldiers.

By right of his marriage with Myram, the student became leader of the band, had not his natural qualifications for the post at once resolved them as to his appointment.   He assumed this position with reluctance.   Heretofore, though he had often acted as a leader among them, and they had learned to look with admiration upon his bravery, coolness, and skill in the hour of danger, yet the student had felt little responsibility, for he was but obeying his leader's commands.   But now he must originate and feel the full weight and responsibility of any affair that they should be engaged in.   However, there was no help for it now; fate seemed to have cast his fortune with these people, and he was already too deeply implicated to dare to think of returning again into the pale of civilized society, had he realized any incentive to do so, aside from the natural disgust he felt at the association in which he found himself with thieves and assassins.

Time passed quickly on with the gipsies in the mountains, and with the villagers of the plain.   The band strolled here and there, now among the thrifty villages, and now hidden in the dreary sierra.   Now joining in some market festivities, and now engaged in some deep and treacherous trick upon the unsuspecting inhabitants.

The student had been with the band now for a period of three years, living as happily with his gipsy wife as could be expected, when it is remembered that one was highly cultivated intellectually, while the other was as barren of principle as she was of refinement.   To suppose that she regarded her husband with the love that first moved her, would be incorrect.   There was nothing congenial between them; there was no subject upon which they felt the least kindred of feeling—what else might have been expected?

The excesses and evil ways of the band grew more and more disgusting to him, until Myram seeing this, by degrees came to hate him as keenly and with more honesty of feeling than she had at first loved. Indeed, a spirit of bitter revenge seemed to grow up in her heart towards one who had never done her a harm, and who, let his convictions be what they might, had always been kind and true to her. At times the student had seriously contemplated the idea of withdrawing himself from the band; but then he remembered his fearful oath, and the force of other circumstances, which seemed to render it next to impossible for him to voluntarily withdraw himself from the league in which he seemed irrevocably entangled.

"There is but one way for me," he mused to himself; "my fate is sealed, and I must go on till fate terminates my ignominious and ignoble career. That I, alas! on whom centred so much of hope and pride, should have come to this? But regrets are useless, and I must shut my eyes and boldly dash on in the course that shall present itself to my feet. I can no longer choose for myself. I am but a poor tool of fortune!"

The spies of the band had reported one day that a rich cavalier and his suite were on the road from Andalusia, and that they would pass the ravines of the mountains soon after midday. They were represented to be a party well armed, but few in numbers, and, according to appearances, would afford a golden prize. Such an announcement, of course, led at once to arrangements among the band for cutting off the travellers, and murdering and robbing them indiscriminately. Without entering into the matter with any particular spirit, the student always led the people on when the proper time came, and directed their movements so as to insure the accomplishment of the purpose that all had in view—that of a successful robbery. Once in the fight, and his blood heated with excitement, the gipsies were accustomed to see him outdo them all in prowess; and this it was, after all, that made them still cling to him, and respect and obey his orders so implicitly, for they felt his superiority.

A few quiet directions, and all the necessary arrangements were made by the gipsies. The band were secreted here and there in ambush, with their firelocks prepared to pick off the outriders and postilions, if necessary, while a small number of the better armed held themselves together and in readiness for a hand-to-hand contest, under the immediate direction of their leader. Thus arranged, they awaited patiently the coming of the expected prize, which was ere long heard in the distance —the heavy rumbling of the carriage wheels, sounding like distant thunder, as it made way over the broken and stony road. On came

the unsuspecting nobleman and his suite, while the gipsies loosened their weapons and felt the keen points of their daggers with glaring eyes. It was many days since a prize had offered, and they were now eager for the prey.

"Fall back!" said the calm, stern voice of the student, as their impatience had led a few to step in advance of him; "it will be time sufficient for you to advance when I give you the order."

The foremost ones fell back at this rebuke, as though they had been children.

When the expected party did appear in sight, they proved stronger in number than had been represented to the gipsies. Indeed, it was evident at once, that the contest must be a severe one, but those dark spirited rovers of the land only looked at their leader's eye, and they were decided. The fact was, that the approach of the contest animated him, and he was no longer the supine, indifferent being that he seemed in the camp. He appeared to have suddenly grown taller in stature, and larger in size; his eyes were full of fire and defiance, and resolution was written in his firmly compressed lips. His orders were issued with calm self-possession, but breathing authority in every tone, while success seemed to await upon his every direction. It was now that his followers looked upon him with feelings almost of awe, obeying his slightest order implicitly.

A sudden bend in the road, as it wound through the mountain gap, brought the carriage and its outriders upon a short plain of level ground, and there the gipsies attacked them. They were not unprepared for a scene like this. Indeed, the character of the times and the route were too well known for them not to have made all convenient preparation to guard against such an attack.

"Cut the traces and dismount those postilions," said the leader to his men, as they rushed upon the devoted cortege; "down with them all—spare none that resist."

With a wild, peculiar cry, as well known among the gipsies as the war-whoop among the American Indians, the dark skinned banditti rushed upon their prey.

The first onslaught was a fierce and fearful one. Traces were cut, and the mules set loose from the carriage—postilions knocked on the head—outriders cut down—horses disabled or driven off—and blood caused to flow like a rivulet, until no further resistance was offered. The victims were conquered, and the prize was won. But the gitanos had not bought the victory cheaply, for more than one of their number had bitten the dust, and were bleeding from deep and dangerous wounds. The nobleman's followers had fought bravely, and scarcely one had yielded until overcome by actual force of arms.

There was a pause now—the fighting was over, and the combatants could look each other silently in the face. The heat of the contest over, their vengeance against each other seemed also to have in part subsided. It was then that the student, with a drawn sword, reeking with the blood shed in the fray, threw open the carriage door, and demanded of those within an unconditional surrender.

In the vehicle there were three individuals —two ladies, one of whom had fainted, and the third person was that of a grey-haired cavalier, who seemed to be too much overcome by ill health to have attempted anything in his own defence during the encounter, and who now languidly reclined against the back of the carriage. His silvered locks hung about his cheeks, and he looked up languidly as the door opened by his side.

But what caused the leader of those desperate people to start back with such a look of horror, and gaze within the vehicle like one half mad, and to close the door again so suddenly?

There was a pause of death-like stillness while all awaited his movements—his followers wondering at the strange mood that seemed to have possessed him so suddenly.

After a moment more of silence, he turned among his people, and in a voice that no one dared disobey, he ordered the prisoners to be released, the horses and mules to be replaced at the carriage, and the postilions and outriders once more to mount, all of which was seen, on the part of the prisoners, with astonishment; and on the part of the band, with a dogged sullenness, which foreboded little short of open mutiny itself. But the eye of their leader was upon them, and full well they knew that no one among them could handle his weapons like him; and his nature, too, they had learned full well, knowing him, when aroused, to be a perfect lion. His orders having been obeyed, he signified to the postilions to drive on; and turning to his followers, said, as he saw the restive character of their features, and their impatience of the restraint he put upon them—

"Fall back! Upon your lives advance ot one step towards that carriage; it is my will, and he who tempts me, shall be made an example for the rest."

"Shall we not revenge our own comrades?" said two or three of the foremost of the gipsies, as they pointed to the dead bodies of their brethren by the road side.

"An equal number of them have fallen also, and this was a contest of our own making. Back, I say! or by this light I will slay a score of ye!" They knew the quick and true hand he bore, and they feared him.

"Will you let this chance escape us, out of some womanly freak of your's?" said Myram, now for the first time appearing, and drawing to her husband's side.

"I have spoken, Myram; let there be no words between us. Yonder people must go from here as they are," said the student, in a tone that even she did not care to question.

Thus the carriage drove on with its maimed and crippled followers, and the gipsies stole sulkily away to their tents upon the mountain's side, to discuss and wonder over the events of the late contest. Not so with Myram. When she found herself once more alone with her husband, she said—

"You are no longer with us, but against us. I have seen it long, and now all know it as well as I do myself. This deed shall be avenged upon you, aye, bitterly—even though I should be the only one in the band who has the courage to punish you. From this hour we are foes."

"As you will," said the student, who turned away from her like one who felt a total indifference to threat or approval; and in this mood he struck into a dark path which he followed alone, seemingly wrapped in deep and absorbing thought of some matter that moved him greatly.

The old cavalier, whose carriage now rolled over the mountain, little thought that he owed his life and release to his own son; for the invalid in that carriage was the old Don Francisco Alvarez, and the student was his only son, now the leader of the strongest band of gitanos that scoured the roads between Andalusia and Toledo; and wondering at his strange fortune, the cavalier, too, went on his way.

The gipsies, of course, knew nothing of these facts, or they would not have so wondered at his conduct. As it was, led on by Myram herself, they at once set about to mutiny, and in some way to get rid of their leader. Myram boldly advocated his death, and at once—to be accomplished while he slept. But there was not one of them, bad as they were, that would consent to his blood being shed—for was he not, like themselves, a gipsy, a gitano, and a brother of the long-reverenced league? Had he not been initiated? "No, no—his life is safe!" said they.

MINNETTA DISPLAYS HER SKILL IN HORSEMANSHIP

CHAPTER VII.

Strength of the gipsy league—A slave sold to the Moors—A Moorish girl—The barb and his rider—The trackless desert—Conscience amid scenes of guilt—The gipsy grip.

"Comrade, your hand,
We understand."—*Bohemian Girl.*

THOUGH, as the gipsy said, their leader's life was safe, and no gitano would shed his blood, still this last act had so enraged them, that they resolved to get rid of him in some way. The most active agent who secretly sought to revenge herself against him was Myram. She did not leave any means untried to incite the hatred of the band towards him. The very fact of her estrangement from him, and the little he seemed to heed it, vexed her beyond measure, keenly touching and wounding her pride.

So binding are the oaths of fidelity towards each other which govern the gipsies, and so fearful the self-invoked penalties for the breaking of any article of their strange league, that, notwithstanding the constant though secret efforts of Myram, still not one of them would consent that his life should be sacrificed. To her it was a bitter rebuke, for she heeded no tie, no obligation—seeking only to satisfy the vengeance she had sworn.

An opportunity at last presented itself, and was quickly improved, whereby the gipsies could, without the shedding of blood, get rid of their leader. One night the band had encamped opposite the Moorish coast, and after the student had fallen asleep, and was completely off his guard, he was seized by a dozen hands at once, bound by direction of his wife, and carried across the waters, where he was sold as a slave to the Moors. This being accomplished, the gipsies placed Myram herself at their head, as queen of the tribe.

Among the Moors a strange and new life awaited the former leader of the gipsy troop. He had fallen into the hands of an officer of the emperor, whose station gave him no small importance; and this official, seeing in his slave an extraordinary degree of intelligence and acuteness, took pains to instruct him in their language, and also gave him a post of trust, and one that drew but little upon him for physical or mental exertion. Fully appreciating these kindnesses,

the slave found in them an incentive to strive and please his master; and thus he became doubly valuable to him, though he was careful never to lose sight of his single purpose, to escape on the first favorable opportunity that presented itself.

Unfortunately his master's daughter—a fair and noble-looking girl—was struck with the melancholy face and fine figure of her father's slave. On his part, the student had no heart for love, and yet he was forced to receive, in the most grateful manner, the profuse, yet delicate kindness of his young mistress; but it was only because he dared not offend, or perhaps in part, that he might, through her, gain more liberty and freedom from his master. And this, in fact, was the case, for at the daughter's solicitations, the Moor permitted his slave to ride now and then upon the horses of his stable, and to any moderate distance from the walls of his own house. This was a precious boon to the slave, as we shall eventually see.

"Tell me again of the mountain fastnesses, and the fertile plains of your country," said his master's daughter, to whom he had before spoken of Spanish scenery. "You know so well, too, of those wild tribes, the gitanos, and speak of them as though you had lived in their midst," continued the girl.

Then the slave would depict the wild and beautiful pictures of his native land, but always with averted eyes, for he dared not look upon one so lovely and so kind, when he felt that his one hope in life was now to escape from her country and her side. He was too generous-hearted to encourage the feelings he could easily detect in her kind actions, or to pleasure his own pride by winning an affection when he felt that he could not honestly return it.

With an undefined plan of escape in his head, he had singled out and trained a steed from his master's stable, and had so accustomed the animal to his voice and hand, that it obeyed him like a dog. It was one of those full-blooded Moorish barbs that have been so famed in song and story. He knew very well that his only hope of escape lay in the endurance and speed of this animal; for, in pursuance of his purpose, he must cross alone one of those trackless wilds of the country that were attempted with reluctance by the natives of the country themselves, even when well provisioned and accompanied by every necessity. But he had a stronger incentive than that which tempted them to cross the desert; it was not traffic and love of gain, but to obtain that boon so sweet to everything that nature has given life to—liberty.

To attempt this wild tract or desert, he required no little calculation and training. The geography of the country, as rudely laid down by those who attempted the subject, had been carefully studied by him, and he had also possessed himself of a small pocket-compass—a most invaluable assistant to his proposed object. However necessary it might be, yet he felt that he could carry but a very small portion of food with him, especially as he remembered that he must fill his garments, as far as possible, with barley for his horse, since the way would afford him scarcely a mouthful of food, and that of the poorest kind of herbage, while the horse's subsistence was a matter of as much importance as his own. After arranging these things to the best of his ability, and keeping every necessary article all prepared and within reach of his hand at a moment's notice, the time for action at last arrived, and the slave, scarcely expecting to succeed, made the final attempt to escape.

He really hesitated for a moment whether he should not return and bid his master's daughter farewell. She had rendered herself so kind and gentle to him, that he really would have delighted to give her a brother's kiss—to have bidden her a brother's farewell, with earnest thanks for the flowers she had strewn in his rocky way. Gratitude is so natural to the human heart, that it is not strange that the slave hesitated, even when his foot was in the stirrup, while his breast was moved by those true and noble promptings of his nature.

Singularly enough, at that moment the object of his thoughts, all unconscious of the feelings that were moving her father's slave, and as little suspecting his real object, appeared at a turret window, and their glances met. It was the first time that the slave had done it so boldly—so feelingly; but her modest token of recognition was returned with a respectful earnestness that she could not but have marked in one so guarded heretofore. She even waved her scarf in her thoughtless satisfaction, as she saw the slave's graceful and tender signal.

In a moment more, with a flood of contending emotions at his heart, he had mounted his barb and ridden leisurely away, as he was often permitted to do, until he reached the point from whence a bold push must be made, and then, at a signal from his rider, the fleet animal sprang off with the speed of the wind!

It was not long before he was discovered by the Moor's household to have absented himself, and pursuit was made after him in force; but the fleetest horse in his master's stud was beneath him, and he feared not, now that he had obtained such a start of his pursuers: the enemy he had now to contend with was the trackless and sandy desert. He held on and on, until the weary animal was like to fall from every exhaustion, when the rider dismounted and refreshed him with a draught from a wild, uncleared spring. He washed his limbs, and dashed the refreshing liquid up his nostrils, and groomed him with the utmost care, before he ever thought of his own physical wants. Then he gave him all he could spare of his little bag of barley, and after permitting him to rest for an hour he mounted once more, and consulting his compass and the stars above him, pressed on his way again, though this time at a more moderate pace than before, and with an easy rein upon his horse.

Day after day that horse and rider wended their way over the desert tract, subsisting upon a mere handful of food per day, and often without water for many long hours at a time. The barley was all gone, but a few dates remained yet, and these were equally shared by horse and rider; while now and then, when they chanced to find such a spot as afforded a little green herbage, it was added to the dumb animal's repast, and perhaps some dried fruit that had ripened upon stunted trees, and fallen to the ground, served to sustain life in the person of the fugitive slave. Then they would struggle on once more in their weary flight.

At length despair seemed to have filled the student's heart; many hours had passed since either himself or his faithful horse had tasted food or water; the sandy and trackless waste was about him; the night, with its refreshing dews, had come and revived them both a little; but holding on his north-western course by the compass, as long as he could urge his horse forward, both at length sank to the ground, and it seemed as though they must die. The poor horse's tongue hung parched and swollen from his mouth, and the rider was so athirst and hungry as to be forgetful, at times, of all things around him. Delirium was approaching!

The night breeze had freshened over the sandy waste, and its cooling zephyrs fanned his heated forehead, when suddenly the horse struggled to his feet, tossed his head and pricked his ears with an instinct and stimulus that his master could not mistake. Some good fortune was in store. He secretly prayed that it might be water that the horse had scented on the cool wings of the night air, and struggling to the saddle once more, he gave the horse his head, though he struck off in a course at right angles with that which they had travelled all day. Fresh vigor was in the animal's limbs, and he almost bounded forward, until, through the dim starlight, there appeared one of those green isles of the desert, a spot scarcely twenty rods in circumference, where a cool spring burst forth from the ground, and watered the roots of date trees heavy with fruit, and the rich soil that was rank with herbage.

It was two whole days before he could make up his mind to leave this fairy spot and launch once more into the trackless desert. Oh, how sweet was that spring of water! how luxurious those dates! and how refreshed was his noble barb by the green herbage and clear water! But after laying in as large a supply of these things as it was possible for him to conveniently carry, without retarding his progress, he again started on his way.

At last, when nearly all hope and power of exertion had left both horse and rider, they come out on the country bordering upon the Mediterranean, and soon beheld the bright waters of that noble inland sea. Here the wanderer found himself opposite the Italian coast, and parting with his faithful horse to a good master, though not without a sigh, he was conveyed to Naples by a fishing craft of the Levant. Poverty-stricken and a homeless wanderer, he made his way on foot once more towards the borders of Spain, and entered its boundaries with a throbbing heart, and almost trembling, too, with various emotions, as he wended his way towards the city of Logrono.

It was five years since he had left his home to go as a student to the institution of Salamanca—five years since he had seen the city of his nativity—five long and weary years since he had been disowned and discarded by his father, Don Francisco Alvarez. His way led him through the very mountain passes he had commanded—the road where his voice had led on his fierce followers to bloodshed and robbery, and where he had so singularly met his father amid the carnage. No wonder that his steps were hurried and irregular here —no wonder that he covered his face with his hands, and hurried on more quickly as he passed some spot more familiar than the rest, mnemonised, perhaps, by some fearful and bloody struggle.

But he was repentant now; he had expiated his crimes in tears of blood, while the suffering and trials through which he had passed had humbled his pride, and, indeed, nearly broken down his spirits altogether, young and buoyant as they naturally were. All this was not without its chastening influence.

Other roving bands were here now, and he was not permitted to pass over the route unchallenged, poor and miserable though he was, and humble as he appeared in his tattered garments. They seemed at first to think him a spy, and even laid violent hands upon him, and brought him as a prisoner before their leader.

"Whence come you, stranger?" demanded the count of the band, sternly.

"From beyond the mountains in Italy," answered the weary and hungry wanderer.

"And whither would you go, that you cross these hills to-night?"

"To seek my home and early friends in Logrono," was the honest reply.

"But we hold domain here," continued the leader, "and tax those who pass these roads, to support our dignity and state. Canst thou give us a ransom to free thee?"

"I have nothing—nay, even now I perish with hunger," answered the weary traveller, fantly. Then starting as though some sudden thought had struck him, he addressed the gipsies in their own tongue!

"Brother," instantly responded the leader, "you should have spoken before. There is food and a welcome for you here; we ask no more—from whence you come or whither you would go. There is our hand, with the gipsy pledge, it is always faithful to the league." As the rough gitano spoke, his whole manner became changed, and no brother could have been kinder in his greeting than was he at that moment.

"I take the pledge, brother, as freely as 'tis generously given," answered the wanderer, as he pressed the count's hand, and gave him back with interest the gipsy grip.

After being refreshed among these people, he went on his way in peace; and such was the binding force of the gipsy league, that he was not even asked one question of his purpose. He knew the pledge: that was enough!

CHAPTER VIII.

The traveller at his journey's end—The old man's story—Bitter repentance—Sweets of domestic bliss—The picture reversed—A new channel for love—Father and daughter.

"His warm but simple home, where he enjoys,
With her who shares his pleasure and his heart,
Sweet converse.—COWPER.

A FEW days more of wandering brought the weary traveller to the city of Logrono. As he drew nearer to his native place, he found that the few years which had been so full of hardship and experience to him, had also brought great and important changes to those who had been left behind. The streets and houses, though in fact, but little if any changed, yet seemed to him to be so strangely altered, that he gazed upon them with wonder. It is thyself that is most changed, Don Francisco!

Pausing in the square near his father's house, he addressed a citizen who seemed at leisure there. He was an old man, but seemed to be well informed of the progress of events.

"And the old Don Francisco Alvarez," continued the wanderer, "who lived in yonder palace—how fares it with him and his family?"

"Don Francisco Alvarez! Why thou art a stranger to ask such questions. He died these twelve months back," answered the old man.

"Indeed!" mused the wanderer.

"Aye, fully a twelvemonth since."

"And the Signora Alvarez?"

"Followed close upon her lord. 'Twas said that an undutiful son hurried their grey hairs to the grave. He left them suddenly, and was never seen after."

The student leaned sadly upon his staff, with an aching heart at what the old man told him.

Mother and father were indeed both gone to their final resting-place in the chapel vault, and the house of Alvarez was without a representative. The officers of the crown had already held it for some months, awaiting the passing of the necessary period, as legally designated, before the property should be confiscated, and then revert, according to the laws of Spain, to the crown. His appearance was most opportune.

The broad estates and the princely house of Alvarez were thus jeopardised, when its sole heir, the wandering student, gipsy, slave, and almost beggar, came within the city gates.

Of course the appearance of a legal heir stayed all proceedings at law, save those that were necessary to instal him as the possessor and representative of the property and the name.

The first duty performed by him who had so wandered from the right path, yet who had already so bitterly suffered for that evil course, was to fast and pray long and seriously for absolution from his many sins; and conducting his penance after the dictates of the church in which he put his faith, he believed himself at last forgiven, and at any rate, was a new, and far better man. He now found the rest and quiet that his spirit so much needed, and sought in worthy charities to relieve the weight upon his conscience.

With his new position came a desire for that quiet domestic happiness which the heart craves as it grows more advanced in experience and years, and finally seeking one of his own rank and standing, he wooed and won her, bearing her to his home a wedded wife. The world seemed to open anew to him now; he truly loved, and was as earnestly beloved in return. There was no one in Logrono who knew the dark secret of his five years' absence, it being generally believed by his friends that he had fallen into the hands of the Moors while travelling in their country, and had been retained as a captive among them. There were indeed many truthful circumstances to corroborate this supposition, besides the story which he had himself given out to that effect, in order to silence all further inquiry.

His knowledge of the Moorish peculiarities, and of their tongue also, was an evidence that would have been sufficient to show his stay among them to have been of not a very brief period.

The wife he had won was a gentle and beautiful flower; all confidence, all trust, and she loved her lord with her whole soul. They were inseparable, ever together, and never tiring of each other; participating now in this gentle and pleasing occupation, now in that, ever finding in each other fresh cause for love.

Thus passed the smooth current of their lives, until Heaven sent them a new tie still more nearly and dearly to unite them—a fair and beautiful daughter. But, also! as is too often the case, the precious gift was at the expense of her own life, and a few weeks of lingering fever laid her to rest for ever!

This blow was keenly felt by the husband; more so, perhaps, because he seemed inclined to consider it a punishment sent by Heaven to avenge the many sins he had committed. In this light it was not without its chastening influence upon him, and for nearly a year he saw no one but his confessor.

The infant, in the meantime, that it might enjoy the benefits of a foster-mother, was carried to an humble but comfortable home, a league from the city walls, where Don Francisco, after the period of his self-imposed confinement, visited it daily. He transferred all the affection he had borne the mother to her tender representative, and he loved the child almost to idolatry. In this course the child seemed to thrive and grow up, until old enough to leave its borrowed mother, and once more return to its father's halls in the city.

Time passed on, and the child grew apace, under the solicitous eye of the father, who, though poorly calculated to guide its tender way, yet bent pliantly to the task. It was a striking picture to see that stern, brave man, who had known such strange adventures, who had led on men fiercer than the wolves to slaughter their fellow-men, who had suffered such vicissitudes, and who had afterwards repented his mode of life so deeply, kneeling there beside that little one, and teaching it to lift its tiny hands in prayer!

And oh! how that little innocent loved him in return, nestling in his bosom, and sleeping there with a conscious security and delight, that won the parent to never-ceasing thankfulness to Heaven.

At length, feeling his own inability to direct and guide his child's education, and form her manners, as well as realizing that it was his duty to make as goodly a home for his daughter as lay in his power, Don Francisco once more made up his mind to the purpose, and married again. He chose with discretion, as he thought, being honestly actuated by the motives we have described, choosing a lady of gentle blood, and of nearly his own age. He married her to obtain a protector and counsellor for his child, not for love; but the disposition which had seemed to him so gentle and winning before the marriage ceremony, now that the honeymoon was over, turned to gall and wormwood. But there was no help for this; and Don Francisco was resigned to his fate, although his purpose, so far as his child was concerned, was quite frustrated, or nearly so.

Sometimes Don Francisco thought to himself that the infliction of this step-mother upon himself was but another deserved punishment sent upon him for the past, and this made him patient.

Isadora, the child of his love, grew up beautiful and accomplished, with far more strength and vigor of constitution than her mother had possessed; and though, perhaps not quite so gentle and lovely in person, still bearing, as a natural inheritance, all the peculiarities of a Spanish beauty, and all the warmth and vigor natural to her race; the rich profuseness of raven hair, the large dark eye, the voluptuous lips, and the olive complexion, that go to make up the Spanish brunette. Her father watched the development of his daughter's mind and person with a jealous eye and growing pleasure, while he regarded her at each returning birthday with renewed interest and love. It was only in relation to her that he ever confronted or disputed with his wife, but when Isadora was concerned, the signora no longer dared to interfere, or openly to oppose his daughter's simplest wishes, though she strove to annoy her in secret.

Still too young to mingle much with the young cavaliers, yet Isadora's charms were known and fully appreciated, and her health was drunk by many a gay gallant at their nightly revels. When she rode out to hawk with her father among the hills, she was sure to meet a score of these young bloods of Logrono, half of whom already swore by her beauty, and wrote sonnets on her eyes, while the elder signoritas envied her this homage, and strove to find fault with her face and manners. To Isadora all this was nothing; she heard perhaps, now and then, by some means or other, of the feelings that were expressed against her, but she cared as little for these censures as she did for the praises of the cavaliers. The fact was, she seemed to be singularly domestic, and to find more pleasure and satisfaction at home in her father's hall than any where else, and expressed no desire to mingle with the world without doors.

As she was still so young, Don Francisco did not particularly regret this, never doubting but that in due time her taste would change with ripening years, and she would be as gay as the gayest, and a peerless belle.

But as time progressed, Isadora still retained her domestic feelings, never stirring abroad without her father, and then only at his solicitation. She seemed to be only happy when at home and by her father's side, and the town's people were wont to call her playfully, Don Francisco's shadow. Her father could not but love her all the better for this evidence of affection, and still doted on his child. No hour was too early for him to be by her side, no hour too late for him to administer to her pleasure. Now he read to her from those old records of mystic lore, in which he loved to revel, and now he listened to her sweet voice in song; now he told her of some Moorish legend he had learned across the water, and now of some hardship, perhaps, that he had encountered in the desert, until she wept and hung fondly about his neck. And then he would almost exhaust invention to create fresh amusement and pleasure for her.

"Nay, father, you humor me too much," she would say, parting the hair upon his brow, and looking up with loving eyes to his face the while.

"Not so, my child," he would answer, returning her gentle caresses, "or if I do, Isadora, I cannot help it, when I remember how dearly I loved thy mother."

"Alas! that she should die so young," answered his daughter, tearfully. "It would have been so sweet, so very sweet, to have loved a mother."

"Love thy father instead," Don Francisco would say, drawing his dear child closer to his side. "Let me fill the place in thy heart that thy mother would have shared."

"You are father, mother—all to me," she would answer, with a kiss upon his noble forehead; and laying her head confidingly upon his breast, she seemed content and happy.

Isadora's heart was like ripe fruit that needeth plucking. It was full of tenderness and of love, and longed to pour its wealth of devotion upon some dear object. This feeling found vent in her love to her father; a pure regard, that we would not contaminate by any alloy; but, as Isadora knew so little of the wiles of the heart, while you and I know so much, we must find for her a reason that

her bosom swelled so inordinately with sighs, and why her eyes oft sought the ground in silent contemplation. We do not mean to say that Isadora was in love, else she would have known it herself, but we do mean to intimate that she was slumbering over a very Ætna of affection and tenderness, that was ready at any moment to burst forth with overwhelming impetuosity.

In short, Isadora was beautiful, Spanish, and eighteen—three items that might be most literally interpreted thus, Love, passion, and romance.

This was the history of Don Francisco Alvarez and his family, up to the time when our story opens, and matters were precisely in this condition on the night when the gipsy trio attempted to enter the house by stratagem, as we have before described, but in failing to accomplish which, they left their agent, Minnetta, behind them, at the mercy of the household they would have robbed.

The lord of this house, Don Francisco Alvarez, was the same student and wanderer whose history we have told you in the preceding chapters, and whose adventures have been related, in order to place our story rightly before you. Then he was a young, gay, and thoughtless student; now his hair was beginning to be silvered in its texture, and there were manly lines in his brow, and furrows in his cheek, though scarcely fifty years had yet rolled over the period of his birth.

It will be remembered that we left Don Francisco and Isadora on the evening when they had been watching the singular movements of the gipsy in the dim moonlight of the old store-room, and now having brought the reader up even with the thread of our history, we will refer him to the next chapter for a continuance of the varied events that make up the story of the Gipsy Daughter.

CHAPTER IX.

Leman Louvelle, the humble secretary—Unconscious love—The gipsy daughter—Wiles of the heart—The troubadour's song of humble love—Its effect—The die is cast—Too late to repent.

"Oh, there's nothing half so sweet in life,
As love's young dream."—MOORE.

WE must ask the reader to remain with us for awhile in the family of Don Francisco, where we would introduce him more intimately to the feelings and character of its inmates.

Don Francisco's secretary, Leman Louvelle,

was humbly born, but having at an early age been placed under the care of a friar of San Filippe, he had contracted habits of study and a love of art and science, that made him ever after a willing and industrious student. It was these qualities which had at first recommended him to his noble master as a secretary; and faithfully had he served Don Francisco during seven years, when a leaf was opened in the book of his fate that very nearly affected not only himself, but another of the characters of our story.

The secretary was a person of fine figure,

but less handsome physically than intellectually. His person was slight and delicately formed, and his features radiant with intelligence. There was a slight shade of melancholy observable upon his countenance, but it was perhaps rather the effect of thoughtfulness and study, than of any real sorrow that he carried in his breast. There was that truly delicate and commanding air about him that intellectual culture rarely fails to impart; and he was altogether one of that class of persons that one is apt to regard with interest and respect.

Leman had been entrusted with the tuition of Isadora in several branches that he seemed particularly well fitted to teach, and this had necessarily led them to be much in each other's society. One of these studies related to chirography; and in teaching her this delicate and beautiful art, it was often indispensable that he should gently guide her hand over the paper, indicating this mode or that of producing the characters upon the spotless page. To say that such contact did not thrill to his very soul, would be to make him out an anchorite; but yet he was too wise to shew this. It would have been his ruin to evince the feelings that struggled in his breast towards his lovely charge.

A true sense of honor led Leman fully to realize this, and he was consequently reserved, sensitive, and delicate in everything that related to Isadora, while she was all freedom and purity, untrammelled by the least reserve. Secure in her high position and rank, she felt no delicacy in calling upon Leman Louvelle at her will; for was he not her father's paid secretary—was it not his duty to serve her? It was his calling, his acknowledged occupation.

This occupation had long since become a pleasure, rather than an ordinary duty to Leman—a recreation instead of labor; for he served Isadora Alvarez with his whole heart. No duty prescribed by her was too onerous, no wish she expressed but it became his ambition and his joy to accomplish. He had no purpose, no object in life that was not framed with especial reference to pleasing her; and thus it was next to impossible that she should feel otherwise than satisfied at everything that the secretary performed for her, be it what it might.

Leman was himself but little more than twenty years of age, impressible and romantic, and it might have been anticipated, long before the event had transpired, that he would love his beautiful young mistress, in spite of his humble rank and position as a hired dependant. It was impossible for him, with his keen perceptions and full appreciations, not to feel the power of her charms, and to almost worship her innocence and trust in him. This was but natural. He could not look upon her without feeling his heart overflowing with love, nor hear her voice without its sweet tones thrilling to his very soul. Of course all this was in secret, and the more powerful, too, for being suppressed.

On her part, not one thought of this character ever entered the head of Isadora. She had been educated and brought up in a manner to feel the pride of birth and position, and though she favored the secretary in all things, listening to his directions with pleasure, while she could brook restraint from no one else, and even looked forward with delight to the hours she should pass with him, still she never thought of love—it had never crossed her mind for one single moment; and had it done so by any strange freak of fancy, her proud spirit would have frowned down the idea at once. How was such a thing possible? Was she not the daughter of the noble Don Francisco Alvarez, and was not Leman Louvelle but an humble secretary? The thought of love in this connection could scarcely be imagined under such circumstances. No;—we do her but justice in saying she never dreamed of such a thing.

The secretary, on the contrary, had analyzed his feelings; he knew and fully realized that he loved this beautiful daughter of his lord,—aye, with an intensity of affection that knew no bounds; but at the same time he knew his love to be so hopeless, that he almost trembled to acknowledge it even to himself. Yet ever uppermost in his heart as it was, he was compelled to ponder and dwell upon it often in secret, but without one single ray of hope. He performed the duty apportioned to him with scrupulous care and faithfulness, never once indulging in a single expression that might betray his love to Isadora. He was strictly conscientious in the matter; and had she even given him ample opportunity to divulge the one great secret of his soul, still he would have remained silent.

Now, on Isadora's part, without knowing it, she really loved the secretary; but his duty was received so much as a matter of course, and his company was always so much at her command, that she had never known what it was to desire his presence and not to have the wish gratified. She had never suspected the true character of her feelings towards him, nor paused to consider but that the same relationship would always exist between them that now so well satisfied her. Perhaps the fact of her wishes in the respect of com-

ABDUCTION OF MINNETTA.

manding the secretary's time as she pleased, had prevented her from ever asking herself the question why she desired to be so much with him, and what the nature of her feelings towards him really were.

True, at this stage, had she thought that her heart was weak enough to love one so far beneath her in blood and rank, her pride would have prevented her from ever beholding him again. But from the causes which we have shown, she remained totally ignorant of the tenderness that lurked in her heart.

It might be wondered at that Don Francisco did not himself discover something of all this; but the same causes that acted upon Isadora, in preventing her from the discovery, in part also acted upon him. The idea of his secretary being so bold as to lift his eyes to *his* daughter—the representative of his proud old line, was really too absurd in his eye to call for a moment's thought. Besides, Don Francisco had of late found great delight in study, and in deciphering old manuscripts and translating ancient documents. His early knowledge of languages gave him a taste for this; and, aided by the family priest, he passed many hours of the night, as well as the day, in this occupation. Thus, perhaps, he was less likely to observe the intimacy that existed between Isadora and the secretary—an intimacy which, however, in outward appearance, evinced no impropriety to the most scrutinizing—it was too insidious in its operation.

When Minnetta, the gipsy girl, came to be her daily, nay, almost hourly companion, she soon detected the fact of Isadora's heart being already filled with tenderness, if not with actual love, for the secretary, though unconsciously on her part. The gipsy life had taught Minnetta penetration and judgment, and she readily discovered that which Don Francisco himself was blind to. But with a natural delicacy and caution, she said not a word to Isadora upon the subject; and when the secretary talked to her with more freedom than he would dare to do to Isadora, because Minnetta was nearer to him in rank and blood, still she pretended not to understand his allusions.

Led on to speak more plainly than he would otherwise have done, by this assumption of dullness on the part of Minnetta, Leman Louvelle told her of feelings that he would hardly have dared to utter to himself when alone. And still the gipsy girl was silent— her policy was clear. It would not do for her to know the state of his heart, and she had better discernment in the matter than the secretary himself. With a most wonderful knowledge of human nature, and the wiles of the heart, that nothing but her roving life could, at her age, have imparted, Minnetta was enabled to read the hearts of both Isadora and the humble secretary, and to understand them, too, far better, as we have said, than they did themselves.

In the meantime, Isadora's father was not blind to his daughter's future prospects, though he discovered not the present workings of her heart. He had already admitted to his house a young and gallant cavalier, named Hernandez Montedore, heir of the broad domains that abutted on his own estates, and whose father favored the acquaintance. Indeed, it was understood already between Don Francisco and his neighbor, Hernandez' father, that their estates should be united by these children. This mode of settlement of marriage purposes, being conducted entirely by the parents, was by no means unusual, and in this instance the two young persons understood very well in what relation they stood to each other.

Isadora had quietly acquiesced in her father's wishes, as it regarded receiving the attentions of her future husband with due respect and gentleness, but she thought little, and seemed to care less, for the subject, seeking to pass her time pleasantly with her music, and the instruction she received from the secretary. Of course the young cavalier, Hernandez Montedore, could not be blind to the beauty and intellectual attractions of Isadora, and he paid her those cheerful and pointed attentions which might have been expected under the circumstances.

"Leman, I tire of these lessons," said Isadora, half pettishly; "go bring thy guitar, and sing to me. One can't study always—it is dull work."

"As you please, my lady," replied the submissive secretary, yet pausing with his eyes upon the ground, as though some inward feeling belied the words he spoke.

"Well, Leman, why do you hesitate?" asked his mistress, watching his movements. "I would hear thee sing, and bring with thee thy guitar. Dost understand?"

"Yes, my lady; but your father would, perhaps, rather I would instruct his daughter, than to have me sing to her," answered the secretary, in a tone of respectful reproof.

"Nay, if it be so unpleasant to thee to touch thy guitar for me, I will not request it again," said Isadora, in a half-vexed, half-pouting tone of voice.

"My lady!" said the secretary, raising his eyes, and saying as eloquently as they could express the thought, how unspeakably happy he was to do her will in everything.

"Well, well, I did not mean to reproach thee. Get thy guitar, Leman," answered his mistress, turning away from his eyes, as though she almost feared to meet their glance.

It was not often that the secretary dared to raise his eyes to hers in that way, nor did he ever do so unless surprised into the act, as he had been now, by her gentle tone of reproach. As he turned to obey her bidding, he felt that he had been imprudent. He could not trust his soul, even through his eyes, when he was in her dear presence. A few more such scenes, a few more such glances, must have inevitably betrayed to Isadora not only the state of her secretary's heart, but also the true promptings of her own bosom. A repetition of the scene might have unmasked to her her own heart.

Something like a faint blush stole over her fair young cheek even now, as Leman Louvelle left her. Was it at some half consciousness of the truth? It is hard to say, for she tossed her little foot, and turned over the leaves of a book with hasty impatience, until, in a moment, the secretary returned, bearing his guitar, and seating himself at a respectful distance from her side, prepared his instrument.

"What shall I sing to thee, my lady?" asked the secretary, respectfully.

"What thou wilt, Leman; choose for thyself and for me," was the answer.

Some strange infatuation seemed to possess the secretary, and he struck forth into a wild Spanish legend, that was entirely new to Isadora, telling how an humble page had loved in secret the proud lady whom he served; and how, for years, he kept his secret, but still loved on; and how, at last, love, which levels all rank, made them one!

The story, which we have told in brief, was given in all the force of the poet's colors, accompanied by the secretary's skilful hand and fine voice, added to which he sang with a feeling that was almost electrical; and, as he ended, Isadora, who had been weeping, rose quietly, and sought her own apartment.

Leman Louvelle almost trembled at what he had done—but it was too late to repent.

CHAPTER X.

The young cavalier, Hernandez Montedore—The gipsy daughter and her heart—The equestrian party—A declaration of love—Isadora and Leman Louvelle.

"When love's well timed, 'tis not a fault to love!
The strong, the brave, the virtuous, and the wise,
Link in the soft captivity together."—ADDISON.

THE fact that Hernandez Montedore was conceded on all sides to be the future husband of Isadora, was perhaps one very good reason that he was not particularly scrutinized as to his regard for her, by the many visitors that frequented Don Francisco.

The visits of Hernandez were constant, and rendered most agreeable by his numerous manly accomplishments. Isadora, Minnetta, and himself, joined by Don Francisco, often made up a cheerful party, either for an equestrian trip among the hills, as a hawking party, or some game within doors—and thus the hours passed agreeably with all, and Don Francisco's fireside was a most happy one.

Hernandez Montedore paid perhaps more particular attention to Isadora, than he would have done, had not both seemed to realize that this was expected of them; but the penetrating and anxious eye of the secretary had marked them well. He said to himself, "She loves him not, nor does he warm towards her as a true lover would do: Hernandez loves not my beautiful mistress." This thought made Leman most happy.

The heart of the gipsy daughter was not all this time inactive, but was beating warmly within her bosom. Of all the young cavaliers that frequented Don Francisco's house, she enjoyed the earnest attention of Hernandez Montedore the most, though neither he nor Isadora were aware of the fact. Experience and early education had taught her caution as well as penetration, and she found but little difficulty in hiding the true feelings that actuated her towards Hernandez under a playful and thoughtless manner. They were necessarily much in each other's society, oftentimes alone; and it was impossible even for a less discerning person than the gipsy girl, not to perceive that the young cavalier regarded her with earnest admiration, and also to understand how easy it would be for her to fan that little flame into a burning light.

Minnetta was not blind; her heart was sensitive; her appreciation keen. She saw all, knew all, as far as a natural inference might be drawn from the devoted attentions of the young cavalier.

But let the gipsy girl's early life have been what it might, she did not in any degree lack a spirit of native delicacy, and a true appreciation of justice and propriety. These traits had been, in no slight degree, redeemed from the weeds that her former associations had caused to spring up about them. Two years' residence among the most polished circles of the Spanish city, and under the tutelage of Don Francisco and the friar, who taught Isadora also in many branches, had so materially changed the gipsy daughter, that her own people would scarcely have known her, could they have met her then face to face in their own camp.

The attention that Hernandez Montedore had bestowed upon her, and the intellectual endowments that he evinced in his communion with her, had led Minnetta to extraordinary efforts in the mastery of her studies; an incentive that she hardly needed, for she had shown a natural adaptation and taste for these things, that had at the outset elicited the warmest praise of her good old instructor, the friar of the house of Alvarez.

With his cultivation of her intellectual capacities, and with the corresponding development of the better nature of her heart, it was not strange that Minnetta felt a degree of principle, as it regarded encouraging the attention of Hernandez towards herself, when she knew so well that it was the settled purpose of her kind patron, Don Francisco, to marry his daughter to him, and indeed that this compact had been agreed upon many years since by the respective parents. And yet the thought would sometimes cross her mind of the secretary and his humble love, and the fact, also, of which she was well satisfied in her own mind, that Isadora, without knowing it, returned the silent yet deep regard of Leman Louvelle. We say she could not but think of this sometimes, while in secret she dwelt upon her own responsibility, and the peculiar situation in which she found herself.

It was very natural that the gipsy girl should seek some excuse for the regard and love that was daily growing more and more deeply rooted in her young heart; and the discovery of Leman's love was a perfect god-send to her, inasmuch as it relieved her conscience of such a weight in the affair of her own regard for Hernandez.

When they flew their hawks, or dashed over the roads on horseback together, the secretary was almost always of the party, and it gradually came to be the most natural thing possible for Hernandez to seek the side of the gipsy girl, and for the secretary to be summoned to that of Isadora. And yet Don Francisco never once suspected the true state of affairs, as it regarded Isadora's heart. Indeed he considered his daughter's engagement with Hernandez such a settled and certain thing, that he never even recurred to it in the way of question as to whether there was a possibility of her ever disappointing his plans by preferring another person.

Such a state of affairs, however, could not long continue. Two ardent hearts, either in the case of Isadora and the secretary, or that of the gipsy girl and Hernandez, must speak out the true promptings that actuated them, either sooner or later; concealment, under the circumstances of the case, could only be temporary. Minnetta thought the old friar, who had an eye for everything, understood them all long since; but if this was the case he said nothing, and after all it might only have been the gipsy girl's imagination that accorded him this penetration.

"Minnetta, you hold that horse in most wonderful command," said Hernandez Montedore, as they were riding side by side, one day, with Isadora and the secretary a little way behind them. "Don Francisco told me yesterday that he is the most spirited animal in all his stable."

"I have ridden from a mere child, and have been taught to control the most vicious animal," replied the gipsy girl, "without accessories of saddle or bridle either."

"It must have been a strange and romantic life that you led with that wild tribe," said he, in a tone partly interrogatory, for he knew very well of her former history.

"Strange, perhaps; but yet I can remember that I was very happy with the band before I knew the luxuries of civilized life," replied Minnetta, with a deep sigh.

"And why not?" continued the young cavalier. "I can imagine not a little delight in the wild freedom and unrestrained purpose of a gipsy life. There is much to love in it after all."

"Oh, there is indeed!" answered Minnetta, with marked animation. "Nature is so beautiful when seen and enjoyed in the open air, and when living in a state nearest approaching to herself."

"And yet you were never designed for a gipsy, Minnetta," said Hernandez, tenderly, guiding his horse still nearer the side of her he addressed.

"And pray, why not?" asked Minnetta, carelessly. "Born and bred in its peculiarities of life, I knew no other, until Don Francisco so kindly befriended me."

"Ah, but you are above the race, Minnetta, in natural delicacy and intelligence. Your true-heartedness could never admit you to the performance of the vile deeds the gitano's life is made up of."

"Do you really think so?" asked Minnetta, archly; "or is my gallant cavalier only paying me one of those empty compliments that are so frequent in the society of the noble?"

"Nay, upon my soul! I feel sincerely what I have said, Minnetta; and," he continued, as he guided his horse quietly still nearer to her side, "much more than I can tell you."

"Steady, steady!" said the gipsy girl, speaking to her high-spirited horse, and patting his glossy neck, as though she understood not any particular allusion in the remarks Hernandez had made.

"You know not how long I have wished for an opportunity to tell you of my true feelings, Minnetta," continued Hernandez, still pressing his suit gently, and keeping close by her side.

Minnetta answered not.

"Do not pretend to misunderstand me. I know you will forgive and listen to me," he continued. "I can no longer bear to keep this burning secret locked within my own heart."

The gipsy girl's cheek became crimsoned, for she knew not what to answer—what to say. She felt that Hernandez was about to utter that which would both render her happy, and pain her too? but yet she could not give utterance to the word that prudence suggested, and to ask him to pause with her where they were until Isadora and the secretary should come up. She could not frame the speech to ask him to do this, though her sense of duty and propriety both pointed to this course, and so they rode on still, until Hernandez had said enough to show Minnetta that he loved her tenderly and most devotedly. The die was cast: he had spoken.

Minnetta had felt that Hernandez loved her; in her heart she had realized this sometime since; but never until now had that regard assumed such tangible shape; never before that hour had she listened to such tender expressions of attachment from him, or indeed received aught at his hand, in word or deed, that might not have been the prompting of a mere friendly or brotherly regard on his part towards her.

"You make me no answer to what I have said to you, Minnetta—have I displeased you?" asked her companion, as they rode quietly side by side, after a few moments of silence.

"Displeased me? Oh, no! no! But we had better not speak upon this subject now," she said, timidly, while she looked back as though she wished Isadora would join them.

"Why not answer me now, Minnetta, and place my heart at peace?" he whispered.

"Spare me, Signor Montedore; there is so much that I might say; such strong reasons that I might adduce why your esteem and regard should be bestowed in another quarter."

"I know very well your meaning, Minnetta. Isadora is apportioned to be my bride; but I love her not, and feeling thus, she can never be my wife. True, my father and her's intend it, but it cannot be."

"Ah! I know that Don Francisco has set his heart on this engagement for years, and I would not be the means of disappointing one hope of his, even to ensure my future happiness for life. He has been more than a father to me."

"Say, Minnetta, were this objection removed, would you look upon me with the same feelings that I have avowed towards you?" asked Hernandez, earnestly. "Would you then return my love?"

At that moment Isadora came dashing forward, just in time to relieve Minnetta from this most embarrassing scene, to the no small chagrin, however, of Hernandez himself.

That night, when returned to the spacious halls of the house of Alvarez, Hernandez Montedore sought a quiet moment to draw the arm of the gipsy girl within his own, and to lead her to a part of the colonnade overlooked only by the moon. It was a fitting hour and scene, and here he again spoke to her upon the subject, which was evidently growing every hour to be of deeper and more absorbing interest to him. He told her that from the first time of their meeting he had loved her in secret, and that from that period until the present his love had gone on increasing, until he could no longer keep it a secret from her.

The gipsy's downcast eyes and heaving bosom, told how that acknowledgment of love was received by her. It needed no words to tell her regard for the young cavalier; he could read it in her looks too plainly to doubt, and taking her unresisting hand within his, he swore to love her, and her alone, for ever.

Hernandez was honest and true in his regard, and his words carried their sincerity with them to the very heart of Minnetta, whose soul gave back its silent, yet eloquent response.

On his part, the young cavalier felt that Minnetta was no common being. Beautiful, almost beyond comparison, delicate, intellectual, and yet fresh, as it were, from a wild and romantic life, that had imparted an interest to her that was really fascinating,

She had been through a fiery ordeal of exposure, and had come out of the test free and unscathed, proving how strong were the natural instincts of her nature, for good. He loved her for the very hardships and deprivations that she had endured from childhood, and in her presence, so far from feeling any degree of superiority, he felt that intellectually or otherwise, as it regarded judgment, she was his superior.

Minnetta stole to her room, after she parted from Hernandez on the corridor, to still the flood of emotions that now filled her bosom. As she passed by the grand reception hall, she beheld Isadora there, listening to the secretary's voice and guitar; and with this picture impressed upon her mind, she sought the privacy of her own room. Here she bitterly censured and blamed herself a thousand times: but for what she knew not. No art of her's had distracted the love of Hernandez from Don Francisco's daughter; that love, however grateful to her heart, had come to her free and unsolicited. This her own heart told her.

"Shall I firmly resolve never again to see Hernandez?" she asked herself; "give way to my sense of duty to Don Francisco's wishes, and thus remove the only barrier to the union of his child with her father's choice? Shall I do this, and be miserable and broken-hearted; shut myself up from the world and him whom I so dearly and passionately love? Oh, I cannot, cannot do this!"

Thus the gipsy girl would reason with herself; and then recalling the scene of the secretary and Isadora together, she would smile to think that at any rate she was doing her friend's heart no ill, for it had never felt a glow of passion for any one but Leman Louvelle.

CHAPTER XI

A morning scene—A wild gipsy camp—An important character—Revenge in a gipsy's heart—The student's gipsy bride—Contrast in situations—Illustration of a gitano's breakfast.

"True, they have vices—such are Nature's growth,
But only the barbarian's;—we have both."—BYRON.

THREE years have elapsed since the night when our story first commences. The grey of morning was merging itself into broad day, and the sun was already high enough to light plain and hill-top. The fresh air, still impregnated with the night dew, was clear and bracing; and those whose duties called them abroad, seemed to feel the tonic of the atmosphere, and move more sprightly and prompt than was their wont at mid-day. The lowing herds wended their way to their daily pasturage, and the busy scenes of the day about the rural districts began to unfold themselves. Here were pretty Spanish maidens, in their national costume, bustling about the doors; and here the husbandman harnessing his mules, or clearing up his yard.

At this hour, on a small plateau of land, without the walls of Logrono, and just a stone's throw from the broad basin and natural springs that supply the town with water, there was a gipsy encampment. The band might have numbered sixty, or more, and was composed of both sexes, presenting the usual tattered and forlorn appearance of the roving tribes of that period. At the hour when we present them to the reader, they were preparing their morning meal; and large pieces of undressed meat, and cakes of ground barley, were baking before open fires upon the ground, while hungry faces and rolling eyes were impatiently awaiting the time to appease their appetites.

In one of the largest tents were seated two figures—the one that of a woman, somewhat advanced in years, her companion a man of middle age, dark and forbidding in countenance—as his tribe nearly always are. The two were evidently discussing some point upon which they could not exactly agree, while the woman's perseverance seemed to put her companion at fault as to the enforcement of his own purpose. They appeared to bear the relation of husband and wife to each other, and spoke without reserve.

"Is not the folly of this enterprise already plain enough before you?" said the man, impatiently; "for, even if we succeed, we shall but get possession of the girl, and how will that make us any richer?"

"It is not gold that I want," said the woman, with a brooding expression upon her dark countenance; "not gold, nor silver, but something better than both of these—*revenge!*"

"Now, I tell thee, continued the man, earnestly, "that this is a foolish business. What have we to revenge against Don Francisco Alvarez? Simply his foiling our attempt to rob him, three years ago."

"So much alone is known to thee," replied the woman; "the past is only known to myself. Think you I had no other purpose than to procure gold on the night when we wished so much to enter his house, and put Minnetta through the iron bars of the window?"

"I thought it was gold we were after," replied the man, carelessly; "you told me so, and I believed you. You said you knew where it was kept, and could put your hands upon it."

"True, true, I did tell you that, and we were after gold, but that was your part of the booty. I sought not such trash as that, but something that is far sweeter to me."

"Has the cavalier, Don Francisco, ever wronged thee, that this grudge should be so bitter and lasting?" continued the man, evincing considerable interest in the expression of his companion's face.

"Wronged me! Aye, bitterly, deeply wronged me! But no more of that now, Rio; I have come here for revenge, and that I must and will have, even if I overwhelm the whole city in my vengeance."

"You talk bravely," said her companion, smiling with an expression of sarcasm on his features; "We are but a handful in all—they are thousands, and well disciplined."

"True; but are we not near the fountain and springs that gives them all drink?" asked the woman, with a most demoniac expression upon her evil face.

"What of that?" said the man, quickly, as though he half understood her meaning.

"Have we no such resort in time of need as the *Drao?*" she half whispered, in reply.

"The Drao!" repeated her companion with a shudder, that showed that the gipsy had referred to some terrible and fatal expedient, that caused even his mind for a moment to revolt.

"Ay; are you a gipsy, and know not the effect of that agent of our race?"

"I know its effects but too well," said the man, turning away with strong distaste at the subject. "Let us talk no more about such a purpose as that."

The woman uttered some muttered expression of contempt at her companion's cowardice, as he turned away, and betook herself to arranging her morning attire.

Doubtless, ere this, the reader has discovered in the gipsy woman, Myram, who had been the wife of Don Francisco, when, as a wanderer and an outcast, he joined the band of gitanos in the mountain passes of Spain. The same wild, revengeful, and turbulent-spirited creature, through whose means, twenty years before, he had been sold into Moorish slavery,—the same Myram, whose strange romantic beauty had captivated his heart when he was a prisoner, where he saw no other type of her sex on whom he could look with pleasure, and who had loved him, too, for a brief period, until she found him wanting in those fiercer and more unprincipled attributes, which force of habit had taught her to look upon as not only manly and requisite, but also necessary to make up the character of one whom she could love.

We say, this strange, dark woman, who sat there thus moodily brooding on revenge in her tent, was the same untamed gipsy girl who had been Don Francisco's wife twenty years before, among the Toledo passes, and with whom he had wandered to the very sea-coast of northern Spain. She who had sustained towards him the tenderest relationship of which our life and associations are susceptible; but which, among our rude and uncultivated race, is a tie put on or off at the pleasure or convenience of either party; this woman, we say, like an evil spirit, had pitched her tent once more by the walls of Logrono, to seek revenge.

In the twenty long years that have elapsed since she met with him who has been once her bosom companion, she had changed but little. Her figure, even in youth, was of unusual size, and had now grown still more colossal in its character, while her face was prematurely interlined with wrinkles, the natural result of constant exposure, and oftentimes of great physical suffering from hunger and pain. She was evidently the queen of the band who were encamped about her, and he with whom she had been talking of her purpose, though he was nominally her husband, was evidently as much under her control as any other member of the band.

"Forget him, or the past! Never!" mused she, when she found herself alone once more, —"I have seen much—aye, enough of life, and if need be, I will sacrifice the few remaining days that I might wander upon these hills and plains, to satisfy this burning thirst against him and his. Rio's womanly soul trembled at the mention of that last resort. What care I! My single hand could accomplish it! We will see—we will see!"

Becoming excited by her own thoughts, the gipsy walked back and forth in her tent with long strides, and seemed to chafe and fret in spirit like some wild animal in a showman's cage. She had evidently wrought herself up to a fearful state of excitement, by long dwelling upon her imaginary wrongs.

With the tenacity of a North American Indian, Myram fostered her revenge against

Don Francisco Alvarez. Had he been in reality the poor and forsaken being she had supposed him to be, when she sold him so treacherously to the Moors, her vengeance and hatred would doubtless have ended there; but when chance discovered to her, not long after his return to the halls of his father, who he was, and that he who had kept their whole band under control by his very voice and eye, and who, by his superiority of spirit, had often quelled their fiercest moods, was once her husband, who had led them so often on to robbery—and had fought with them, hand to hand, against their prey; we say, when she found that the poor wanderer, who had been, and had done, all this, was Don Francisco Alvarez, now revelling in luxury and wealth, while his former companions, and she, who had once been his wife (this was the most sensitive point of all), starved or begged on the open moors, then her heart became so embittered and revengeful, that it could scarcely contain itself within the bounds of reason.

At first thought it would seem as though she had already sufficiently harmed him, when the part she had taken against him is remembered; but she was operated upon by peculiar circumstances.

True, she had already done him evil enough —had shewn her hatred towards him when he was utterly powerless, and had remorselessly sold him into the bitterest of servitude; but all this weighed nothing with her now; it was the realization of their present contrast in situation that so keenly embittered her feelings. When, with the girl Minnetta, she had failed to enter Don Francisco's house, she had been driven by the authorities, upon his information, to leave the neighbourhood, and had been closely pursued by the government soldiery; but the noble cavalier himself little knew to whom he was indebted for the proposed robbing, which he so narrowly escaped. As Myram and her band at that time had fallen partially under the observation and displeasure of the authorities, they had not dared to return again to these parts until the lapse of the time specified. But their purpose, or rather that of Myram, was not forgotten; it was religiously treasured up and consecrated by a vow, to redeem which, she had once more pitched her tents in the outskirts of the city.

Rio, the gipsy, after leaving her side for a short time, had again returned. He evidently had no taste for the business which brought his mistress and wife to this spot.

"As to your revenge, Myram," he said, "that is no account of mine, nor of the troop generally; and then as to getting Minnetta again, I can see no great object in that either."

"No great account?" answered the gipsy, seeing that she must adopt a different course in order to bring about her purpose. "Was there ever one of us who won so many broad pieces at a market fair as did that girl?"

"True, she did dance well, and played the tambour with skill and neatness."

"Who ever resisted her appeal for silver after a dance upon the green sward? Of no great account, Rio! look at our treasury now —it is at a low enough ebb. Minnetta would fill it again."

"Ay, if we could keep her; but that girl's got a taste for luxuries, and a few notions picked up from the gentry, and I never saw one return to us worth the keeping."

"Leave that to me," said the woman; "I trained her from childhood, and I will take care when once she is among us again, that she forgets nothing, or the practice of it, that I have taught her."

"As you will, Myram," replied the man, with a sort of dogged submission to her arguments; "but remember, I like not this busiuess, come what may of it."

"Peace, croaker! you have said enough," replied Myram, angrily, as she turned away from him. "What would our people come to, with such a leader as thou art? Alas! for my brave old father."

"Get Minnetta back if you will, and then let us away from this neighbourhood," replied the man.

What relationship really existed between Myram and Minnetta—if indeed, there was any—was evidently unknown even to him by her side, but if her conversation was any criterion to judge by, she bore the girl little love at least, speaking thus of her long absence from her and from the troop, as being a pecuniary loss only, declaring that she was the best of the whole band on a gala or market day. Though the reader will observe that this reference, after all, was made more to excite the cupidity of Rio, and enlist him in the proposed plan, that the gipsy seemed to have submitted to him, as to a second attack upon Don Francisco's house.

Could any one have seen the under vestment of the gipsy queen, as she gathered her garments now more closely about her, they would have been able to judge somewhat of her character.

A short hanging sword by her side was hidden by the ample folds of her outer dress, and the handle of more than one broad-bladed Toledo knife, of finely-tempered steel. About

THE GIPSY QUEEN ASTONISHES FRANCISCO.

her neck might have been seen a metallic whistle, evidently designed as a signal or alarm-call. Her feet were covered with raw hide sandals, heavy and coarse, designed for service, not beauty, while on her head she wore a slouched hat, like that worn by the men of the tribe, save that in its front was a richly set garnet stone, holding in place a single feather, much like the style of a bonnetted Highland chief. It was the only distinctive mark she wore about her person, though her bearing and size marked her from all the rest.

The rude meal was prepared now, and throwing themselves in groups upon the ground, they were served with meat and bread from the fire. Wooden bowls were the only dishes used, and the meat was divided with their fingers and the aid of a sharp dirk-knife, such as they all wear at the girdle for offensive or domestic use.

The scene was a true picture of their desolate and roving character, and illustrated the secret charm of their life—a wild and reckless independence, congenial with their habits and temperament.

CHAPTER XII.

The gipsy daughter's early life—Scenes of the castanets and tambourine—The strange mono-mania—A sad young heart—The generous-hearted cavalier—Isadora and the humble secretary.

" Hath not custom made this life more sweet
Than that of painted pomp ?"—*As You Like It.*

UNDER such tutelage as Myram was like to give her, it was strange that Minnetta had not grown up like herself, full of wickedness and evil propensities ; but the truth was there had ever been in her bosom a guardian angel to prompt and direct her feelings; and her own native spirit had kept her pure at soul. Through all her wanderings, and during the entire period, from her infancy to the hour when she was taken as a prisoner by Don Francisco, her purity of soul had never once been violated. True, the gipsy queen had taught her many a wicked trick, for Minnetta then knew no better than to follow her directions. But those stains upon her were such as could be easily washed out again, and her subsequent life under her protector's roof, had now entirely obliterated them from her character, and she had at once clothed herself with self-respect and modesty.

This band, thus encamped near the city, was the same with whom the gipsy daughter had roamed over the fertile districts of Valencia and Murcia, where they found not only the populous town and thrifty inhabitants, upon whom to exercise their art, but where also, when shelter from justice or pursuit was necessary, the lone waste and dreary sierra were always near at hand. Still better for their predatory habits and purposes had proved the district of La Mancha, a land of tillage, of horses and of mules, where those dusky rovers of the plain were sure to find ample field for occupation.

But better than all had been to them Andalusia, with its three kingdoms, Jaen, Granada, and Seville, a part of which, at that period, was still held by the swarthy Moors. Andalusia, the land of the proud steed, and the stubborn mule—the land of wild wastes and savage sierras, and of fertile and cultivated plains. They loved this land and cherished its beauties in their rude songs. It was here that Minnetta had grown up among the tribe—it was here, among its gay villages and market towns, that she had danced to the merry chimes of the castanets, or the bolder tones of the ringing tambourine.

No wonder that she could not efface the memory of those scenes from her heart.

With these people she had slept in caves and beneath the open sky—was now an hungered, and now filled to surfeiting ; with them her baths had been the showers from heaven, her music the thunder, and her light the forked lightning. Their rude, unseemly tent had been her gilded palace, and the broad, outspread scenery, decked by Nature's dainty hand, had been the Flemish pictures that the gipsy girl had known.

Is it to be wondered at that Minnetta, now enjoying all the luxury and refinement of Don Francisco's house, should often revert to these scenes, and lose herself for hours in the memory of the past ; nay, that, overcome by the fascinating charm that had fixed them in her heart, she should sometimes secretly clothe herself in her old mode of attire, and once more imagine herself among the scenes and companions of her early days, as Don Francisco and Isadora had surprised her in doing, by the dim light in the old store-room ?

This gipsy passion,—it could be called nothing else,—came so upon the poor girl, that, had Don Francisco or Isadora realized its force, they might justly have feared the possibility of her leaving them for her old associates when the fit should be upon her. There seemed to be magical power in its influence, entirely beyond the control or understanding of Minnetta herself. At moments, all the good counsel and example that she had known under the noble roof where she now found protection, were as nought, their power appeared to be lost altogether, and she seemed to crave her old habits—to long for the gipsy tent, and the open air, as sailors, who have been long at sea, and delirious with fever, have been known to rave and pray for a *green leaf!*

At such moments, when she felt this uncontrollable desire upon her, she would sometimes mount her horse, and with a single attendant, dash out of the city, and over the hill and plain at a speed that would return her spirited animal to his stable covered with foam, while her attendant would declare that his mistress must be mad, for he had absolutely struggled to keep his seat, and her in sight. Had Minnetta been closely observed on such occasions, when the furor of the desire was passing away, it would have been seen that a cold perspiration stood upon her fair brow, and that she seemed like one recovering from a trance, or as though she were awaking from a long and troubled dream, that had wearied her in sleep.

Don Francisco Alvarez, who had been so kind to her, had never lisped to Minnetta that he, too, had once been connected with the gipsy tribes, nor had he ever uttered to her one word of their language, though it was still as familiar to him as the purest Castilian. For the same reason that had caused him to remain silent upon this subject, he never asked her any of the particulars of her former life, or permitted any one about him to do so. He had been prepossessed in her favor, at first by her remarkable personal beauty, and afterwards by the noble qualities that he discovered in her disposition and general character. Then, too, a secret and irresistible influence attached itself to her, from the very fact of his connection with the race, during his wanderings in the years long since past. He could not but treat her with more consideration than he would have done, not knowing the habits and peculiarities of her race in a state of nature.

On her part, the gipsy girl had grown to love Don Francisco most tenderly, for the kindness that he had uniformly evinced towards her, and for the constant interest he had displayed in her studies, and her ad-

vancement in every accomplishment that Isadora's teachers were competent to impart. Every advantage of this character was freely shared wiih Isadora, as indeed was all else, for they lived together as two loving sisters. As it regarded Isadora herself, she could not have been more tender and loving to the gipsy girl had the ties of blood united them.

Thus Minnetta, notwithstanding the fact of her having made her entrance into the house in such a questionable manner, and under such peculiar circumstances, was still most happily situated, or at least she had been most content and happy until the revelations of the past few days, which have already been related. But now that she knew of Hernandez' love for her, she felt an indescribable guilt. Though in reality she was in no wise to blame for the course that matters had taken, still she could hardly bear to look upon Don Francisco, when she realized that his object in relation to his daughter's fortune, had been frustrated by her.

Her early education had never been able to callous or harden the natural delicacy of her nature, and for this reason she suffered severely, though she uttered no word of complaint, and had no confidant to whom she might communicate the bitterness of her sorrow, and of whom to seek advice; so that, although surrounded with kind friends on all sides, yet Minnetta felt that she was alone in the world. Isadora, who was wrapped up, in a measure, with her own unanalyzed feelings, was not looking upon the gipsy girl with sufficient scrutiny to detect any extraordinary exhibition of feeling, unless it was vastly out of the ordinary source.

It is rare that two young girls of their respective ages can long remain together without opening their hearts to each other; but there were good reasons why this was not the case with them. On Minnetta's part, her feelings as to having thwarted, in a degree, the purposes of her kind protector, would have been reason enough, had she no other, why she would not have referred to the subject of her love for the young cavalier, Hernandez Montedore. And, as it regarded Isadora, her feelings were yet unanalyzed in her own heart, or had she even realized that she loved the humble secretary, still her proud heart would have kept its own secret; for she was proud, not in a way to affect her gentleness of disposition, but on the point of birth and rank.

Minnetta had thought much of her position —she had mused and saddened over it until the traces of her mental struggle were left upon her countenance in the shape of a settled melancholy. She was sitting one afternoon, just at the twilight hour, in the drawing-room, when Don Francisco entered and addressed her:

"Good cheer, Minnetta, what dream you about there, so sagely and soberly to yourself?"

"Dream about, signor, why do you think I am dreaming?" she asked, pleasantly.

"You look as though you were dreaming."

"Do I?"

"You do indeed, Minnetta; and I have marked that you have grown sober and thoughtful of late," continued Don Francisco, as he gently drew the gipsy girl to his side, and placed one arm about her waist.

"Oh, I am not sad," replied Minnetta, striving to appear pleased and cheerful, while she parted the hair from her protector's noble brow, and looked lovingly and tenderly into his face. Nor was this feeling in any way feigned, for she almost worshipped Don Francisco, who had been so good to her.

"You know you are my daughter now; that we have agreed upon, and I shall assume a father's prerogative, and scold you if I see any more clouds on that pretty face."

Minnetta replied not for some moments to his kind reproof, looking the while into his eyes, and laying her head upon his shoulder, for a guilty feeling would creep over her as she thought of her being the means of defeating his long cherished hope in relation to Isadora and Hernandez.

"Ah, signor," she said at last, "you are always but too kind and indulgent to me, and daily place me under obligations that I can never repay."

"Repay! You have a thousand times recompensed me, Minnetta, with your gentle love, for the little I may have done for you. Talk not of payment to me, my child."

"You are so kind," repeated the gipsy girl, nestling by his side as she spoke.

"You do not regret then, Minnetta, that fortune cast you into our hands?"

The true-hearted girl made no reply, but laid her head affectionately upon his shoulder, and could he have seen her eyes, that were hidden from him at that moment, he would have discovered tears in them. If she had so long been a rover with the gipsies, it had not hardened her young heart; that was as true and lovely in its sensitiveness, as those who loved her could possibly have desired. There was not a prompting of her young breast but was as truthful and maidenly as her more fortunate companion's, the kind Isadora.

Aged but fifteen years when she had entered the family of Don Francisco Alvarez, she had now become eighteen, three years having transpired since that, to her, memorable night. In that period, always, saving those times when the gipsy fever came over her, her very feeling had changed, she saw with new eyes, heard with new ears, thought with a new mind, as it were, so different had her perceptive qualities become. Then added to all this she *loved*, and that state of the heart alone opened a new existence to her, causing her to see all things in a different light from that which had dimmed the ideal of the past.

Sometimes, blessed as she felt herself to be in the great change of her life, yet she almost questioned whether she was so happy as she had been before these finer perceptions were developed in her soul.

"When I knew little, I thought little, and performed my daily task with mechanical correctness. But now, Oh, how much, how bitterly I think oftentimes, and how sad am I this very hour," she murmured to herself.

There was not a little reason for Minnetta to feel unhappy, when she fully realized the delicacy of her situation. The facts of her humble origin, and the hateful influences that had hung about her youth, now appeared doubly unfortunate and painful to her, since one of noble blood had told her that he loved her. While she was free and unconstrained in her feelings, she thought little of the past, striving only to improve and judiciously occupy the present; but now everything was changed—all things were seen through a new phase, and she could not help mourning in secret that she was only the gipsy daughter.

Isadora had still eyes and ears only for the humble secretary, although she knew not the secret that prompted her to watch so earnestly for the hour of his coming to her side. It was hardly to be supposed that she should have suspected the truth, his station was so lowly, his manner so subdued and humble, while her own position was scarcely less exalted than that of a royal princess. We say it was not natural for her to suspect the truth, realizing, as she must do at all times, the vast contrast in their relative positions. It would require something extraordinary to remove the veil from her heart, so that with her own eyes she might look in upon its tablets, and realize the truths that were recorded there.

That event must, of course, take place sooner or later, for each day unconsciously her voice grew more and more gentle when she spoke to him, and each day he lingered in her presence with increased but silent delight. By neither word nor deed did he ever betray the least want of that respect which he so truly felt, and which, as her servant, and her father's secretary, he owed to her. The most watchful could find no fault with his deportment.

Still leaving the gipsy band, with their revengeful leader, encamped near the springs that supplied the city of Logrono with water, we must refer to a matter of serious import to our story, that occurred at this time.

CHAPTER XIII.

The fearful accident upon the road—The bravery of the secretary—A peculiar love scene—Leman Louvelle's story—A proud lady's confession—The parting scene.

"Lo! all the elements of love are here—
The burning blush, the smile, the sigh, the tear."—
BAILEY.

AS time passed on, and one event upon another caused Isadora to regard her tutor, Leman Louvelle, with more and more interest, she began at last to have suspicions of the real feelings that moved her heart. The troubadour's story that he had sung to her, was the point from which her understanding seemed gradually to take its start, and herself to turn, though tremblingly, her eyes within her own heart. At first, even to herself, she refused to own the truth, —her pride rose up so strong and bitter in rebellion, that the struggle was fearful.

The full force of her education and entire life were so much against the indulgence of a love for the humble secretary, that whatever her heart might indicate, reason and pride seemed to overrule them.

It was night, and she was alone in her own room. The day had been an eventful one to her, and had raised the curtain from her eyes, and shown her clearly that, in spite of everything, she loved the secretary. She had been in company with her father, Minnetta, and Hernandez, on a hawking party, and, for the first time, had ridden the horse that the gipsy girl had always chosen. Indeed, Minnetta was the only lady that had ever dared to tempt his mettle, and, perhaps, was the only female hand in Logrono who could have curbed and rendered pliant his fiery spirit. This fact being generally admitted, Isadora had determined to mount the horse, and had that day done so, riding him, on a party, as we have said, to the hills. She was quite a mistress of the menage, but not equal to this task.

The horse grew restive and unmanageable at a certain point, and all Isadora's efforts to conquer him with the heavy Spanish curb that was used in those days, proved unavailing, and at length her position became one of great danger, as the horse was on the very brink of a precipice, plunging and rearing fearfully. Leman Louvelle, as was often the case, was of the party—and his was the eye, of course, to first discover his mistress's danger. Death would have been a pleasure to him if incurred in her service, and in a moment he was by her side; by his aid, she dismounted in safety, not a moment too quick —for the next instant both the horse and her faithful secretary were dashed together over the precipice!

This had all transpired in such a brief period of time, that when Don Francisco, missing his child, turned to see if she had fallen far behind, he beheld her with clasped hands standing alone at the edge of the precipice,

Leman was not killed, though his preservation seemed to be almost a miracle; but bleeding, and sorely wounded, he was conveyed back to the city. Weeks had passed since this fearful accident, and Leman had lain upon a bed of harrowing pain, though no complaint had ever passed his lips During that time, Isadora and Minnetta both had attended him with the most unremitting kindness and attention. The secretary, pale from the loss of blood, and weak from pain and suffering, was still now declared to be well enough to leave his bed, and her anxiety thus in some degree allayed, Isadora was now musing alone in the privacy of her own chamber, as we have seen, relative to the secretary.

For days Isadora would not see him at all, either keeping her own room, or managing to avoid his presence in some way, until at last, on one quiet afternoon, they met by accident in the drawing-room. Isadora's cheeks were at once tinged with a color that betrayed her inward feeling, and she could not but start back and sigh deeply, to see the secretary's pale cheek and attenuated form, for she realized fully that the suffering he had endured was for her sake solely.

The secretary paused, and bowed humbly before the proud girl. He could not do less than that, and remained with his eyes upon, the floor, while Isadora bit her lips, not knowing what to say, and almost annoyed by his respectful and distant manner towards her. His cheek was so pale, his air so melancholy and subdued, that Isadora's woman's heart was touched, her sweet lips trembled, and a single pearly tear started down her cheek !

The secretary heard that soft sigh, and, looking up, beheld that tear.

"Lady," said he, almost trembling where he stood, "was that tear dropped for me ?"

"For thee ?" said Isadora, quickly recovering herself, and summoning all the proud spirit that had so long sustained her ; "yes, Leman, it *was*, to think that you should have suffered so much."

"It was sweet, lady, to serve thee in any way, and my lot was enviable."

"Thy promptness and ready aid saved my life, and it is not strange, then, that I should regret the suffering you have endured," continued Isadora, striving to find an excuse for the feelings she had evinced.

"They were lightened by the consciousness that I shared the while your kind solicitations," said the secretary, with his eyes still resting upon the floor, a picture of humble and dutiful respect.

Isadora bit her lips so as to almost start the blood, while she struggled with her own secret feelings.

Both felt the embarrassment of their situation, and neither seemed to know what course to pursue. They presented, as they stood thus together, a striking picture. Isadora's beautiful face, alive with contending feelings, and her bosom agitated to quickened motion ; her eyes now stealthily bent upon the secretary—now averted, as though she feared lest he should detect her thus gazing upon him. But at last she gazed more fixedly at his fine face, and subdued and humble deportment. She could not bear to see him thus, and for a moment the pride that had actuated her own bosom also swelled it again in his behalf. She felt that, intellectually, Leman was her father's equal, and that even the friar of the house, so wise and learned, honored the secretary for his wisdom and attainments. She seemed to consider for a moment that intelligence, not station or blood, is the true attribute of greatness, and to forget the worldly contrast between Leman Louvelle and her own position in life.

The secretary could not move ; he *felt* that her eyes were upon him, though she spoke not : and his own brain was no less actively employed than Isadora's upon the same subject that engaged her.

"Leman, why don't you speak to me ?" said Isadora, at last, with an impatient accent, as she seated herself, and tossed her pretty foot with vexation at the state of affairs.

"Has my lady any orders ?" said the secretary, turning suddenly, though his eyes were not raised from the floor, nor the tone of his voice any the less respectful.

Isadora seemed more annoyed than ever at the studied respect of his manner, and rising hastily, walked away to an alcove of the apartment, and then returning, once more seated herself.

The secretary saw these impatient movements, and hardly knew how to interpret them, though his heart whispered to him that there were warm feelings struggling within her heart for utterance. And so there were, —Isadora could hardly restrain her feelings, and never before had she so struggled with love and pride. Covering her face with her hands, and sobbing like a child, she lost all control of herself.

"Lady, for the love of Heaven, what does this mean ?" said Leman Louvelle, kneeling by her side, and with an audacity that astonished even himself, gently placing his arm about her waist !

This was all that was needed to arouse the dormant pride of Isadora ; that touch of the secretary's arm, the first familiar token that he had ever offered her, was sufficient. The spell was broken,—the proud girl was at once the mistress, and he the humble student. She sprang to her feet as though an adder had stung her to the very heart, and turned coldly and sternly upon him.

"Lady, forgive me," said the secretary : "If for one moment I forgot myself at witnessing thy unhappiness, I pray you forgive me, and I will never offend again."

His instant contrition, and the humble tones of his rich musical voice, that she had so often listened to with secret pleasure, moved her heart again ; and as she looked upon his pallid cheek, and remembered that he was scarcely yet recovered from a nearly fatal injury, incurred for her sake, her pride vanished at once.

"Leman, do not kneel there—you are ill, and should be very careful of yourself !"

A stroke of lightning could not have moved him more, had its electrical fluid pierced his body, than did this sudden change in the spirit that actuated Isadora towards him.

"Ah, lady," he murmured, "it is so sweet to hear you speak thus to me."

"Rise, Leman, rise, and sit thee down on this couch," she continued, kindly.

The secretary did as he was desired, and so changed had his fine intelligent face become within a minute's time, that even Isadora looked upon him with surprise and pleasure. She had always conceived him handsome, and he was remarkably so,—but under the continued restraint that had governed him, she had never seen the light of his very soul burning within his eyes before. She blushed anew as their expressive glances rested upon her own with such tender yet earnest devotion.

"Leman," she asked, suddenly, "are you happy?"

"Happy, my lady? I—"

"Oh, *my lady* me no more, Leman; I cannot bear it longer from thy lips."

"I will be honest, then; until this moment I have scarcely known what happiness was for years."

"And why not, Leman?"

"Lady, may I tell thee truly, why I have been so unhappy?"

"Do, Leman."

"Then it has been for a deep, unutterable, and hopeless love for thee! The more sad that I could never give it utterance, and the more deep because of the vast difference in our stations, which I know separates us as effectually as though the grave itself intervened between thee and me. From the first, I have loved thee with a passion so true, that it has been my sole incentive in all things. When first thy father entrusted thy early lessons to my charge, he forgot, alas! how nearly I was in age to thyself,—he forgot how beautiful and gentle you were, and how young and ardent was his humble dependant and secretary. But I strove on daily, monthly, ay, yearly, to do my whole duty to you; and though only happy when by your side, yet as sacredly holding my peace, and suppressing every selfish motive, as though I had been a stone.

"As years have advanced, and you have grown to the full bloom of womanhood, my heart had almost rebelled more than once, and I then half resolved to tell thee all, pray for thy forgiveness, and then leave this house and thee for ever!—Sometimes a gentle tone, or a kind solicitation in my behalf, has filled my heart with secret joy for days and days, and yet I have never spoken or done aught that did not become thy proud state to hear, and my humble position to utter. I appeal to you, lady, have I ever forgotten the respect due to your rank, or the duty that devolved upon me as a dependant?"

"No, Leman—no!" said Isadora, whose face was again hid in her hands, while she wept.

"At last—and not even then save by the solicitation—I sung a song to thee, a troubadour's song, in which, under the guise of a story, I told to thee my own feelings, and the hopeless love I bore thee. Oh, how my soul longed, when you rewarded that song with silent tears, to pour out its love at thy feet. But habitual care in thy presence had taught me caution, and with a full heart I left thee again. Still the days passed on, and I was often by thy side, until that hour when I was fortunate enough to render you a service, that caused me the harm I have suffered of late. But oh, could you have read the invalid's heart, while you bent so gently over him, and bathed his fevered temples, you would have seen that the joy of your presence and kindness far outbalanced the pain that racked his physical system; and that, spite of all, he was almost too happy!

"And now, my lady, what am I to think of this moment—this scene, to which I have never looked forward? You have been speaking to me as you have never spoken before—you have listened to my story from beginning to end—you do not bid me leave you. Oh, say, lady, what does this mean?"

"Leman, I cannot—cannot speak!"

"Oh, if I rightly interpret this gentleness, those tears, and that modest confession, do not banish me from you yet—let me drink in this delirious joy for one moment more!"

As he spoke he knelt again by her side, and this time pressed her unresisting hand to his lips, again and again. He could hardly believe that all was not a dream,—a fiction of the brain.

"Oh, tell me, lady—speak to me, that I may know I am not deceiving myself," he continued, so earnestly, and so pleadingly, that Isadora, dashing the tears from her face, placed both her hands in his, and said:

"Leman, it is useless to deceive ourselves; I love you!—ay, have loved you long, without, however, knowing that this was the real sentiments that made me seek your society so much. I need not multiply words; if you have felt as you tell me, for so long a period, your own heart will show you that this regard has been mutual, though more unwitting on my part. I need not tell you of my father's plans and hopes, of his pride and rank,—these things you know; and, therefore, Leman, this must be our last meeting, none the less for your sake than my own, for from this hour I am wedded to misery."

As she spoke she rose, and with one gentle pressure of his hand, bade him a tearful farewell, and conjured him, as he regarded her peace of mind, never to attempt to see her more,

"What a Heaven is this to fall from! said the wretched and hopeless secretary.

CHAPTER XIV.

Bitterness of the Signora Alvarez—The two conspirators—The secret panel—The strange and powerful narcotic—The gipsy queen.

"Offend her, and she knows not to forgive;
Oblige her, and she'll hate you while you live."—POPE.

THE only happiness, and indeed of late, nearly all the occupation of Isadora's step-mother, had consisted in unceasing endeavors to annoy both her and Minnetta, though the gipsy girl seemed more particularly to call forth her antipathy and jealousy, from the fact, perhaps, of Don Francisco's extraordinary interest in her, and the uniform kindness he evinced towards her. Signora Alvarez was the first of the household to learn that a tribe of gitanos had pitched their tents near the city walls; and no sooner had she heard of this than she secretly wished that there might be some means devised whereby Minnetta might fall into their hands, and leave her sight for ever, though, under existing circumstances, there was no possibility of such a thing occurring.

Minnetta knew that Signora Alvarez bore her, for some reason best known to herself, a secret enmity, but she did not think that she was half so vindictive as she really was.

In her bitterness, Isadora's step-mother resolved herself to betray Minnetta into the gipsies' hands; yet, how she could accomplish this, without being known in the affair, was a mystery to her, and she passed many sleepless hours in seeking how this might be done. She knew very well how Minnetta had got away from the roving tribe to whom she belonged, and thought that doubtless they would be overjoyed to get her back again, either through mercenary feelings, or those prompted by kindred of blood. In either case her object would be equally well served, and after a while she resolved to put in execution a plan she had formed.

To accomplish her object it was necessary for her to see some one of the tribe, secretly; but by the adoption of means that none but a woman as artful as herself could have thought of, she was enabled to communicate with the woman who led the band, in relation to the object she had in view, and to Myram she unblushingly avowed the purpose and wish that had led to her seeking her presence.

"What would you with me?" asked Myram, coolly, meeting Signora Alvarez at the place that had been appointed, not far from the encampment of the tribe. "There are others of my people who can tell fortunes as well as myself; why do you single out me to meet you?"

"Fortune-telling is not the business on which I come," said Signora Alvarez; "my object is very different from that. I have news to tell thee, and a scheme for thee to accomplish."

"Speak!" said the gipsy.

"First, you must promise me secrecy; that you will in no case betray me."

"Promise! what is a gipsy's word worth?" said Myram, with a sarcastic smile.

"I come not here to bandy words with thee?" replied the signora, with spirit.

"Well, then, if it satisfies you any better," answered the gipsy, "I promise you."

"You know the house of Don Francisco Alvarez?" continued the visitor.

"Ha! yes, what of that?" said the gipsy, changing in her demeanor at once.

"There is a gipsy girl there—"

"I know it," replied the gipsy leader, with a calm, stern smile upon her lips.

"Minnetta."

"That is her name. But why do you come here to speak to me about her?" enquired the gipsy, with her keen dark eyes bent upon the lady with a searching glance.

"She belongs to thy race, does she not?" continued the Signora Alvarez.

"Ay! to this very tribe."

"So much the better for my purpose," said the visitor, with earnestness.

"For what purpose?"

"I would have her again among you, and out of the house of Alvarez," continued the signora. "Ay, and that too, as quickly as the matter can be accomplished."

"Who are you?"

"Signora Alvarez."

"*His* wife?"

"Her visitor almost trembled as she observed the demoniac expression of features that seemed for a single moment to overspread the countenance of the gipsy queen.

"Oh! I understand you are Don Francisco's wife, repeated the gipsy.

"The same."

"And you like not this Minnetta—this gipsy girl?" she replied. "She has made one enemy among you then, at least. Does Don Francisco tire of her also?"

"I know not, nor do I care," exclaimed the

MINNETTA

signora. "It is sufficient that I hate her, and she must leave the house at once. If you will not aid me, others must."

"'Tis well; your purpose shall be served, and with your help I will relieve you of her presence most willingly," answered the woman, with ill-suppressed tokens of pleasure.

"But remember, I am in no way to appear n the affair—you understand?"

"I do."

"Take this key, then," said the signora; "it opens the secret door to the court-yard of the house, four paces from the western angle of the wall. It is so nicely secured and formed in the wall, that unless you are particular to mark the distance, you will hardly discover it."

"Four paces from the western angle of the wall," repeated the woman, carefully, as she counted her fingers, in order to keep the number in her mind.

"Yes; and it leads you into the main court, from whence you can at once ascend to the corridor above, and the fourth door from the head of the stairs, running northward along the passage, is the room occupied by her whom you will seek. You will use all caution."

"I will."

The gipsy marked well the directions she had received, while her eyes gave ample tokens of the satisfaction that she had derived from this singular interview.

"Is the door to Minnetta's room locked?" asked the gipsy, after a moment's silence, in which she seemed musing over the details of some plan relating to the matter.

"There are no locks within the walls," answered the signora, save on the doors that open below the corridor. This key will be all that you require in order to possess yourself of her person. It must be done by stealth, not by the force of numbers—two or three, at most, should be all that enter the court."

"We will be discreet and prompt," said the gipsy; "it is no new business for such as we are. This very night, signora, the thing shall be accomplished."

Thus the two, having accomplished the object of their meeting, separated.

It was about the same hour that night as that in which our story opens, within the city of Logrono, the moon shone brightly, and the stars hymned their silent praise as they had done for centuries before. No one was stirring or awake, save here and there a drowsy night-watch, nodding at his post of duty, or striving to remain wakeful, would pace his narrow limits back and forth several times, only to return still more inclined to give himself up to inviting slumber. The Spanish city was as still as a peaceful dreamer.

At this moment, three persons crept stealthily out from the deep shadow of the moon, and, seemingly, vanished through the stone-wall that formed the outer boundary to the court-yard of the house of Alvarez. Two of these persons were men, the third was a female, large in stature and powerful in frame. It required no second glance to discover that it was Myram, the gipsy. She was faithful to her promise, and her errand there was that which we have already described.

Her companions remained by the secret panel were they had just entered, while she, following the directions which she had received from the signora in the morning, soon entered the apartment occupied by Minnetta. The gipsy girl was sleeping peacefully, but the door left open towards the corridor, and the small loop window opening on the other side, furnished enough of the moon's light to make all distinctly visible within the room, and to enable the gipsy easily to perform her intentions. With a sort of vacant curiosity, she carefully examined the apartment and some of its furniture; but this occupied her for only a minute—she had other and more important business to perform.

Approaching the bedside she gave a smile so perfectly demoniac and fiendish as to seem to obliterate every trace of humanity in her countenance. In this manner she gazed for a moment upon the sleeping girl in silence. Her hands were crossed upon her gently heaving bosom, and a soft, serene, expression of innocent repose rested upon her features, which were almost angelic in their sweetness.

A scene that would seem to be sufficient to call up all of gentleness and kindness that any human being had in the soul, appeared only the more to embitter and enrage the heart of Myram. She stood there, mumbling to herself bitter and revengeful words, and staring with a wild, unnatural glare upon the sleeper. There was no motion, no noise in the room or without, that could be heard: even the breathing of the gipsy girl, as she lay there wrapped in forgetfulness, was so soft and gentle as to emit no sound.

Still the strange dark woman paused and bent over the sleeper, until it seemed as though she was recalling a deep dream of past years—as though her memory became at once painfully burthened in its activity, and, indeed, as though she recalled much that would gladly be forgotten. The sight of the sleeper seemed to have acted as a talisman to conjure up before her eyes the secrets of the past, and it was these memories that led her to pause, and perhaps almost to falter, in the purpose of her visit.

But suddenly starting, she threw off this lethargy by an effort, and remembering where she was, and for what she had come there, and loosing the stopple from an antique jar, which she took from the folds of her dress, she thoroughly saturated one corner of the hanging curtains of the bedstead with the liquid contents of the jar, and then averting, in part, her own face, to avoid inhaling the exhalation, she held the cloth to the lips of the unconscious girl. As she inhaled the strong and pungent perfume emitted by the liquid, she seemed to fall deeper and deeper to sleep, until her breathing was almost imperceptible.

"How like death," said the gipsy, "this is to look upon. How potent. I would not give her too much—no, no, the time has not yet come, not yet, not yet!"

The gipsy listened with her ear to the sleeper's lips, felt of her forehead, and laid her hand upon Minnetta's heart, then, as if fully satisfied that her strange narcotic had produced its desired effect, she wrapped a blanket close about the sleeper, and raising her in her arms, bore her towards the secret entrance of the court-yard with as much ease as though her burthen had been an infant.

"Rio," said the woman, as she laid the body for a moment upon the ground, "bear her gently and quietly to the camp, place her in my tent, she will not wake for nearly two hours; but if I do not return by that time, see that she is closely looked after, and not permitted to leave our quarters.

"Does she not go willingly?" asked one of the men.

"What is that to thee?" said the gipsy, sternly.

"I did but ask," replied the man, abashed at her earnestness.

"Mark well what I have said, Rio, if she wakes before I return."

"I will; but if you have given her of that powerful jar, there is no fear of waking."

"How strong is that smell," said the other, averting his head, as the fumes of the gipsy narcotic rose to his face.

"So we are really to have Minnetta among us once more," said Rio. "Well, brother," he continued to his companion, "take her up gently, for she's a good girl, and we must not wake her."

"Be quick and away," said the woman, impatiently; "this is no place for parleying."

Thus saying, the two men, seeming to understand the part that they were expected to perform, took Minnetta's now helpless form between them in their arms, and bore her swiftly away towards their camp, leaving Myram behind, who seemed in no hurry to follow them.

After satisfying herself that her assistants had made good their escape from the neighborhood, the gipsy paused for a few moments in the shadow of the wall, until some menial, who had occasion to move from one part of the house to another, had passed, and then she arranged the secret door with much care, leaving it in such a condition as to admit of her instantaneous egress if she should desire it.

This being done, she ascended the broad steps once more that led to the corridor, and entering the room from whence she had just taken Minnetta, she sat down, covering her face with her hands, and musing as though irresolute whether to turn and leave the spot, or still further to pursue her vengeance.

CHAPTER XV.

The midnight visitor—The surprise—The strange meeting after twenty years' separation—The attempt at assassination—The silent vow—The secret enterprise.

"Muse not that I thus suddenly proceed;
For what I will, I will—and there's an end."—
SHAKSPERE.

THE gipsy remained in the thoughtful position in which we left her at the close of the last chapter, for a few minutes only, when she aroused and seemed to be actuated by some new purpose. She stole cautiously along the spacious corridor, until she came opposite a door that appeared to be the object of her search, and this she noiselessly opened.

It was Don Francisco's chamber, and as she stepped within, she was startled at seeing a lamp burning at that late hour, and the cavalier himself seated at a table, and poring over some book of interest, in which he had, as it appeared, become absorbed. As the woman entered he looked up hastily, but turned to his book again, as he said:

"Ah! Friar John, are you, too, up at this late hour? But you are welcome, for I have got against some Arabic lines here that puzzle me hugely. Sit down, sit down."

Don Franciscso had evidently mistaken his strange visitor for the good priest who was attached to his household, and who not unfrequently visited his patron at his midnight studies; for Don Francisco Alvarez was a student, and loved to pore over his books, and wander amid the mental paths of recorded lore, that his own library and that of Friar John afforded. In the mean time the gipsy obeyed his desire, and sat down opposite to him, in silence.

"A calm and still night is this, Father John, and there are no revellers to interrupt one," continued the cavalier, still struggling in his mind to conquer the Arabic puzzle.

"Ay, there may be no revellers to break the stilness of the night," said the gipsy, hoarsely, "but there be those abroad, nevertheless, whom you little wot of!"

"There be those abroad I little wot of?" replied Don Francisco, leaning back on his chair, and shading his eyes from the blaze of the lamp, he peered curiously at the supposed priest

"Ay, no priest nor friar am I," continued the gipsy, boldly, from out of the folds of her ample covering, as she rose to her feet and confronted the cavalier.

"I begin to think so," replied Don Francisco, cautiously rising to his feet, and quietly loosening the dagger that was ever deposited within his vestment.

"You know me then, do you, Don Francisco!" said the gipsy, in her natural tone of voice, and with a stern, sarcastic accent in intonation,

"I know you not," replied the cavalier.

"Do you know me now?" said the gipsy, throwing the large mantle she wore away from her face and head, and looking boldly upon Don Francisco as she spoke.

"Myram!" exclaimed the cavalier, with a shudder at the recognition.

"It is Myram."

"Can this be possible?" continued Don Francisco, almost overcome with the emotions of the moment, and covering his face as if to shut out the sight before him, and the memories that crowded to his brain.

"Ay, it is the same Myram, who was, twenty years ago, your wife! She with whom you led the boldest band of gitanos between Toledo and Andalusia—she who has fought by your side, and who has slept and watched there. Your wife! who has starved while you fattened—who has been shelterless while you revelled beneath a palace's roof. You are right, Don Francisco Alvarez, I *am* Myram, the gipsy queen!"

"How found you entrance within these walls—by what means did you enter?" asked the cavalier, still averting his eyes from her face, as though it was pestilential for him to look there.

"That matters not," said the gipsy; "you know that we heed locks and keys but lightly, Don Francisco, and it is sufficient that I am here, without discussing the means."

"And for what purpose are you here?" asked the cavalier, "why have you thus come hither to vex and torment me by your presence?"

"I have come hither for a double purpose; first, to be revenged of you, and afterwards to secure the person of Minnetta, who has been here these three years," replied the gipsy, boldly,

"Minnetta!"

"Ay."

"Belonged Minnetta to the tribe you lead, Myram?" asked Don Francisco, with a sudden interest that it was impossible for him to disguise.

"She does."

"I understand it now," said Don Francisco sternly. "So then it was by your instigation that the girl, some three years ago, at midnight—"

"You need not finish the question. I understand what you would say. It was by my instigation and direction that she came here," answered the gipsy.

With this decided answer, Don Francisco mused for some few moments in silence, during which he went back again, in imagination, to the days when he had been a wanderer with the gitanos, among the mountain passes and fertile plains of Spain. But he was interrupted by Myram, who said:

"When I believed you to be the poor miserable worm we had taken up and fed at first, my revenge ended with getting rid of your presence, and placing it out of your power to again restrain our movements; but when by chance I afterwards learned who you really was, and I considered the cheat you had put upon us, my desire for revenge returned to me anew, and I resolved to have it.

"You were not content with the vile and cowardly trick you played upon me in selling me into that bitter servitude to the Moors?" said Don Francisco.

"Not when I knew to what estate and rank you had risen afterwards," replied the gipsy, bitterly, as she shook her finger meaningly at him before her.

"It is of no account now," replied Don Francisco, calmly, "many years have passed since that time; we have found that our path in life lies in vastly different channels. Have a care that you trespass not upon my way again, or I will denounce you to the authorities."

"Denounce me to the authorities!" repeated the woman, with a bitter sneer.

"I will—both you and your tribe, if you annoy me further."

"Ha! ha!" almost screamed the gipsy, in her excitement. "You talk like a child. Denounce me, and implicate yourself. You will hardly try that game, Don Francisco."

"I defy thee and thy whole race!" was his quick and spirited reply, "and give thee but a moment to escape from these walls as you entered them. After that I will arrest and detain thee."

"Imprison me, Myram—thy former wife, and now a free gitano."

"By the name I bear, I will do it, unless you leave my presence at once."

The dark eyes of the gipsy seemed almost to emit fire, in the intensity of her anger, and she fairly trembled where she stood with excess of passion. Watching her chance, she sprang towards him with a naked dagger in her hand, aiming a blow at his heart: but he had not forgotten the vigor or activity of youth, and seizing the stout and masculine creature before him in a way to render her weapon entirely useless, he cast her from him as though she had been a child. His spirit was up now, and he was not to be trifled with any longer, even by such as she was.

The gipsy staggered to her feet, and seemed abashed at the feebleness of her effort. Muttering some unintelligible expression of bitterness, she paused only for a moment, and then darted away, leaving Don Francisco half in doubt whether he had not just awoke from a troubled dream. It seemed so strange to him to meet that fierce, dark woman again, and under such circumstances.

He waited where he stood for some time, collecting his thoughts, and not a little puzzled at the events of the past few moments; and then remembering himself, he determined to seek by what means the gipsy had effected her entrance. To do this, he summoned Leman Louvelle, and together they sallied forth, and groped here and there for a long time, but to no purpose, for the secret door in the wall was known only to the priest and the Signora Alvarez, who had together used it for some secret purpose.

"Unless by the aid of some person within the house, I can see no way for her to have entered," said Don Francisco to the secretary, after a long search.

"None of the people could be bribed to admit a gipsy," replied Leman, "they attach too many evil associations to them, and fear them beyond all reason."

"True, there could hardly be an understanding between them and my people."

Being at last satisfied that it was by some means beyond their power to discover that the gipsy had effected her entrance in the house, Don Francisco at length gave up the search; but suddenly remembering that the gipsy had openly avowed to him, in their late interview, that her object in coming there was to gain possession of Minnetta, he instantly repaired to her room, to see if she was there, when his worst fears were confirmed by his seeing her bed tumbled and empty, and herself nowhere to be found. He had not brought Leman Louvelle with him to the chamber, but had entered it alone, nor had he said anything to the secretary of his fears about Minnetta; but his resolution seemed instantly formed, and kissing the cross upon his dagger's hilt, he uttered a vow within his soul, in a spirit that shewed at once that nothing, save death, would prevent his keeping.

Don Francisco felt scarely less interested and love for the gipsy girl than for his daughter, Isadora. She had come into his household at the most impressible and interesting age, and he had taken no little pride in his endeavors to mould and form her susceptible mind. She seemed possessed by Nature with so much natural instinct, and such peculiar feelings, that the cavalier found singularly consonant with his own, that altogether he felt drawn towards her day by day, until he really loved her nearly as well as Isadora. And then the artless sincerity with which the gipsy girl returned Don Francisco's love, and the grateful spirit that ever beamed from her eyes upon him for all the uncounted kindnesses that he bestowed upon her, was a cementing power to his own regard for her.

Thus actuated towards her, no wonder that he uttered that vow to release her from the vile thraldom of the gipsy league, or to die in the attempt. That was the spirit of his silent vow.

No one knew the gipsy habits and stratagems better than he, and no one knew better in what way to operate against them. He saw on the instant that the adventures of the night would be followed by a sudden flight on the part of Myram and her band; and he realized, also, how futile were all attempts made to follow them by any organized force. The soldiery they could easily elude and deceive; besides which, he did not care to expose his former life by calling out such aid in his behalf. This, of course, must have been the ultimate result, if he should succeed in overtaking and confronting those whom he had once commanded.

"No, no," said the cavalier, "it is but a simple object, and one that any stout arm, with my experience, should not hesitate to undertake. I will operate alone, and by that reason the more surely."

A slight signal summoned Leman Louvelle to his side, to whom he said—

"Tell my people—and particularly Isadora, that some business has called me away for a day or for a week. I know not how long, but I will return anon."

"Whither do you go, my lord, on such a sudden errand, as calls thee away at this hour?"

"It matters not, good secretary; and with thee we leave all the care of our household. Be trustworthy, and when we return, you will have added another to the many trusty deeds thou hast done for our house."

"The Virgin guard you, signor, for by your look and manner, I fear that there is matter of sad import weighing upon your mind. If it be so, may not Leman Louvelle serve thee more nearly, by following thy steps."

"Nay, good secretary, all will be well, tell this to Isadora, and now good night."

As Don Francisco said this, he grasped his dependant's hand warmly, and turned away.

Returning to his chamber, the cavalier did not lay himself down to rest; he had no desire of the sort; but he silently clothed himself for action. Slipping beneath his vestment a shirt of Milan mail, which he had already tried in the tide of battle on the fields of Arragon, and in his country's cause, he soon completed his attire. It was nearly daylight, however, before he had entirely finished his dress, with sword and dagger prepared for instant use; and as the gray of the morning broke over the city of Logrono, the cavalier wandered forth on his errand alone.

CHAPTER XVI.

"'Twas blow for blow, disputing inch by inch,
For one would not retreat, nor t'other flinch.—BYRON.

THE Signora Alvarez had one other vein of evil which she had lately discovered, and which she had resolved to work. In her watchfulness, she thought that she had discovered, on the part of Hernandez Montedore, a growing partiality towards the Gipsy Daughter, and though she did not herself believe that this was a matter of serious import, or that the young cavalier really had any serious affection for Minnetta, yet the idea itself was enough for her, and she looked about her to see in what place she should throw the flaming fire-brand that she at once determined to light. To hint such a thing to Don Francisco would have been folly, for he would have cast back the insinuation as base and ridiculous, and moreover, she did not care to be brought into collision with him.

She knew very well that Hernandez's father was as earnestly intent upon his son's marriage with Isadora Alvarez as was Don Francisco himself; and that if possible he would be more sensitive upon the point, allowing it to be true, than would Don Francisco, since the latter regarded Minnetta with the tenderest love, while Hernandez's father would consider that his son was to be ruined by his love for a mere gipsy.

One would think that the signora would have been content with the evil she proposed to bring about, as it regarded betraying Minnetta into the gipsies' hands; but no, hers was a disposition that could only find joy in the misery of others, and the more extensive and bitter that was about her, the better satisfied she became. Vile and disagreeable as her disposition was, we have many such about us—almost any community where we chance to find ourselves will afford us a specimen of the same character. Those about the signora, though they accredited to her the true spirit that belonged to her, yet did not think her half so bitter as she really was—

"They did not know how hate can burn,
In hearts once changed from soft to stern."

Seeking the most combustible point, therefore, at which she could light her incendiary fire, the signora resolved, by some shrewdly thrown out hints, to excite his suspicion, and thus lead to that rupture and trouble that was such delight to her. In pursuance of this object, she had met Don Hernandez Montedore the day before that on which she had seen the gipsy queen touching the abduction of Minnetta, and by sly words and hints artfully thrown into her conversation, as though they were but casual remarks, she succeeded in placing the old cavalier upon thorns. It was delightful to her to witness misery in any one, and she enjoyed his perplexity immensely; and while she pretended to soothe his anger, by hinting at the possibility of her being mistaken, notwithstanding what she had seen and heard, she cunningly added fuel to the flame, until, when she left Hernandez's father, he was half beside himself.

When Hernandez met his father, as a matter of course he found him in a great rage, and, to his no small astonishment, was arraigned before him in the light and position of a culprit. But the old lord forgot that his son had inherited some portion of his own spirit and fire, and was not a little confounded by the calm but resolute and unflinching silence that his anger was met with. When at length Don Hernandez Montedore had exhausted his fury as far as to be able to speak in a reasonable manner, he found his son more communicative.

"So you have been overthrowing the plans that I have formed for you, and setting up a scheme of your own, it seems. The lady Isadora Alvarez does not suit your fastidious taste."

"Signor, I do not understand your vague and angry hints," was the answer.

"Angry—angry! Hernandez, do you call me angry, you foolish boy, you; you—you—stupid fellow, do you call me angry?" said his father, growing purple in the face.

"Well, signor, I must say that you have about you every symptoms of such a state."

The old cavalier saw that in his present mood he was not equal to the task of reasoning with his son, and he walked back and forth, at first with an unequal step and angry haste, but by degrees he became more and more composed. It was a process of reasoning within himself, and though he was no less determined than before, he had become calm, and now turned in a very different manner to his son.

"Hernandez, I have reason to suppose that you are neglecting the lady Isadora Alvarez, and the compact which you know I have formed with her father, and are indulging a passion for a nameless gipsy!"

"Signor, who has told you this?" asked Hernandez, now excited in his turn.

"It matters not how I became possessed of the fact, if fact it be."

There was a pause, during which Hernandez said nothing; but his cheeks burned like fire.

"Your face, Hernandez, shows your guilt; I need ask no more."

"Guilt! signor?"

"Ay, guilt,—cool, deliberate treachery to me, and the noble line whose name you bear. Would you debase both me and yourself by pursuing such an affection as this?"

"I can realize no guilt in loving such a being as she whom I love," replied Hernandez, earnestly.

"You boldly acknowledge, then," said the father, "that my supposition is true."

"I do."

"Then hear me, Hernandez," said the old cavalier; "I am advanced in years, but my arm is still vigorous—I am aged, but my will is strong. A few moments since I was angry, I am no longer so—now I am only determined. Now, that which I utter, as I hope for mercy in Heaven, I will keep good—"

"Hold, signor!" said his son, reading the deep resolve and stern unrelenting purpose of his father in the expression of his face, "hold! utter nothing rashly, for rashness begets rashness."

"Do I look like a rash man now, Hernandez?—am I angry or heated?" asked the old cavalier, calmly, as he gazed upon his son. "I see your answer in your face. I am your father, Don Hernandez Montedore, in the calm and full possession of all my reason and faculties, am I not?"

"Signor, yes," said his son, deeply troubled at the aspect of affairs.

"Then listen," continued the old cavalier, kneeling and drawing his sword, the hilt of which bore the universal Catholic emblem of the cross; "I swear before Heaven, that if you wed any other than Don Francisco Alvarez's daughter, with this weapon, and my own right arm, I will take your life!"

"May the Virgin forgive thee for that vow!" said his son; "for in life or in death I am only Minnetta's—and no earthly power shall prevent her from being mine!"

"You know me well, Hernandez, and whether I am one to keep my word or not," said his father, as he turned away from his son with an expression upon his face that showed his will was unchangeable.

The reader may think that the threat of Don Hernandez Montedore was a most preposterous one, such as he could never possibly put in practice; but such forget the character of the times of which we write. They do not remember that the warlike spirit that pervaded every class, and the habit of participating in civil wars, and frequent battles with the predatory bands of the country, when any necessity called forth the citizen to travel upon the roads, all tended to harden the heart to acts of cruelty, and to reconcile the feelings to deeds of violence, and to the resort of extreme measures in almost any crisis.

As to Hernandez, he never for one moment doubted that his father would keep his vow, nor would any one who knew the resolute character and stern pride of the old cavalier. The history of the sixteenth century is replete with stories of fair ladies immured in convents, where they died of broken hearts, because, forsooth, they loved not those whom their stern and proud parents had selected to be their future lords. Nor were the instances few where noble youth had been disowned, or violently sacrificed, for like offences. Violence and compulsion were the characteristics of the times when might made right, and the sword comprised the code of civil law.

Hernandez felt that there was some one who had acted the spy over him, and he was justly indignant at the tattler who had revealed this subject to his father; but it mattered not, now that it was done, who had done it, and as to the Signora Alvarez, she never entered his mind at all as being the medium of his trouble. Indeed, that artful woman, chancing to meet him just before her interview with his father, took unusual pains to appear pleased and flattered by his notice, such was the treachery of her disposition.

The ancient families of high note in Logrono might have numbered perhaps a dozen, who in a measure disputed precedence with the houses of Alvarez and Montedore. As a general thing, the little matter of jealousy between them had only gone so far as exhibitions of neglect towards one another on several occasions, though sometimes the various dependants of these houses, when they chanced to meet each other, dressed in the liveries of the respective houses to which they belonged, would banter words of insult or threats, that sometimes led to blows among themselves, differences that perhaps never reached their masters' ears. Yet more than once, these quarrels had spread so as to draw the various houses into hot controversies, and more than once, too, had led to their resorting to arms in the adjustment of their fancied rights and wrongs.

Such an advent was suddenly brought about on the very day to which we have just referred, and but a few hours subsequent to the scene that we have related as occuring between Hernandez and his father.

One of the retainers of the house of Valesquez had struck, in a banter of words, a follower of the Montedores, and from a single personal affair between the two retainers, by degrees each had summoned aid from his friends, until a score on either side were engaged in a general *melée* or street fight. But finding, at last, that their efforts to injure each other, or settle matters by fisticuffs, were of little avail, both parties retired to reinforce themselves, and also to procure arms, with which to vindicate their respective causes.

As these parties had a second time come together in one of the squares of the town, and swords were flashing and blood flowing freely around, Don Hernandez Montedore chanced that way, when the followers of the house of Valesquez, in their mad fury, one and all set upon him. They were sorry swordsmen, these humble fellows, while Don Hernandez had been often crowned victor in the knightly sports of the tournament, for his skill and bravery at arms. His sword drank blood at every thrust, and his assailants felt that he was equal to a score of them.

But the brave old cavalier was sorely set upon by numbers now, and as this encounter had chanced to take place in the vicinity of the house of Valesquez, the numbers of his assailants were increased every moment, and he found himself at last hemmed it at every point, while his followers were kept from him by encountering the new comers. It was a critical moment, the blood of those who assailed him was up, and in their recklessness, they now boldly sought to take his life.

But at this moment, a shout rose from his followers, and was echoed by his assailants, of "a Montedore! a Montedore!" and he beheld his son Hernandez, whose young and athletic form towered above the *canaille* above him, with his sword flashing like the light, actually hewing a way with its keen edge to his father's side. Another moment, and striking two of his assailants dead at his feet, he leaped before the almost exhausted person of Don Hernandez and with his eyes emitting the fire of rage and daring, boldly confronted the vile band who a moment before had crowded upon his father.

The old cavalier's heart beat quick and earnestly as the young champion stood there life a giant, with the crowd cowering before his skilful arm and brave look. He forgot for a moment his own critical situation in his admiration of his son. While leaning upon his own sword, he panted from every exhaustion at the arduous part he had so suddenly been called upon to enact.

At this moment, the followers of the house of Montedore were greatly reinforced by additions to their number, and their enemies were obliged to retreat; not, however, until

DON FRANCISCO'S ENCOUNTER WITH THE GIPSY.

Hernandez had cleft more than one skull among them, as he pursued their flying steps with his fresh followers, stimulated to revenge upon them the insult and bodily harm they had done his father. Then hasting to his father's side, he aided him once more to the safety of his own palace walls.

The old cavalier, when once seated in his own hall, looked with pride and a loving eye upon his brave boy, and, for the first time, discovered that the blood had stained through the thick doublet he wore, from some wound in his side, and calling him closer to him, he said, with the tenderest solicitude :

"Quick, Hernandez, quick, and see to thyself—thou art wounded, my brave boy, sadly wounded; the blood hath stained now through thy doublet."

"Nay, but a trifling wound, signor; the rascals touched me with their daggers."

"See here!" said Don Hernandez, "quick! dressing here, I say!" he continued, to an attendant, as he opened Hernandez's doublet and discovered the wound, which, though not a dangerous one, was yet severe.

He held him with his own hands, and was as tender with his brave young deliverer as a woman might have been.

"Hernandez, but for thy good sword and ready arm, I had perished. 'Twas thy bravery alone that saved me," continued the old man, tenderly. But then, as if suddenly remembering himself and their late interview, he said :

"Still, Hernandez, my vow is registered in Heaven, touching thy marriage, and I shall keep it to the full extent !"

CHAPTER XVII.

The pursuit—The spy—The dumb friend—The strange monomania—The supposed dream— The infusion of blood—The remedy—The flight —The pursuit—The death struggle.

"Dead, for a ducat, dead !"—HAMLET.

WHEN Don Francisco left his house, as we have described, he was partially disguised, and before he passed the city gates he was completely so. He did not expect to find the gipsy camp where it had been—he knew very well that they were gone already on their way towards some place of safety, best known to themselves, and this indeed was the case ; but, well versed in their craft and habits, Don Francisco soon struck their trail, and pressed on after them.

It was already evening when he at length came up with the band, who had pitched their tents for the night in a grove of woods by the mountain's base, and were now thrown negligently around, resting themselves upon the hard earth after a forced and long march of about six leagues. Don Francisco's tactics were plainly those of cunning, not open force; his single arm would have been nothing against them all, and strategy was his only hope.

He resolved to wait until it should be still later before he ventured upon his disguise to enter the camp. He knew their ways and language so well that he had little fears as to being able to preserve his incognito ; but the most delicate part of his business was as to how he should gain the ears of Minnetta, whom he felt must be with the band, probably in Myram's own tent, if a tent the crazy thing could be called, full of holes as it was, and exposed on all sides to the action of the weather, or any one that wished or dared to intrude.

Don Francisco had sought out a quiet spot that overlooked the camp, where he had thrown himself down to rest, and where he might arrange some plan as it regarded the object that had brought him there. The moon was gradually rising as the night advanced, and throwing its pale, clear light over the camp, revealed everything to his inquisitive eye. While he lay there in ambush thus watching the people below, he heard a slight rustling near him from behind, and the next moment was startled by the forefeet of some animal thrown heavily upon his chest, while he felt its hot breath upon his very face ! His dagger was raised almost as quick as thought, but it descended harmlessly, for the new comer was only Minnetta's dog, who had scented out his footsteps.

Fondling the affectionate animal, which had ever been a favorite of his, he mused on as to how he might accomplish his wish. While thus occupied, he beheld Minnetta herself come out of a tent and gaze about her with singular composure and apparent interest. He even beheld her sit down and freely partake of the rude meal that a small party had prepared. There seemed to be no restraint placed upon her. She moved and appeared like one that was free to do her own will and pleasure. This puzzled Don Francisco ; but he was glad to see that she was not forcibly confined, as his task would be so much the easier as to her removal.

It was after eleven o'clock that night when Don Francisco, after careful examination, boldly walked into the camp and threw himself upon the ground, as though he were quite at home. He had selected the spot where he had thrown himself, because it was near the tent which Minnetta had several times come from and again returned to, and his position was such as to intercept her, should she again come out as she had done, on her way to the centre of the camp ground, where, after gazing at the moon for a moment, she retired. Don Francisco had seen her do this several times, and was so puzzled at her manner, that he looked twice before he was satisfied it was she.

Scarcely had he laid here for a minute when the dog rushed out and fondled and caressed him in his dumb style, so that the cavalier was fearful that the creature, in his kindness, would betray him. But it was not long before Minnetta herself appeared, and as she approached Don Francisco, she did not seem to heed that any one was in her way,—so odd indeed did she appear that he did not speak to her, but watched the strange expression of her eye and her oddity of manner, until she had gone quite past him. There was something about her manner, too, that he had before marked in her, odd as it was, and at last he remembered, as he watched her now, that he had seen her precisely thus, in that dim old store-room, within his own house.

As she returned towards the tent again, he determined to accost her, let her mood be what it might, and in a few moments she drew towards him once more.

"Minnetta!" he whispered.

She paused and started for a moment, as though that voice, even in a whisper, was familiar; but in a moment more kept on, until she was arrested by her name being once more repeated.

"Who calls me?" she asked, in a low voice, turning towards Don Francisco.

"A friend, Minnetta; draw near to me, quickly. Come, there is no time to lose, follow me at once out of the camp, and I will conduct you in safety to our home."

"Home! Is not this my home?" she asked, almost wildly, as she looked about her in such a way that Don Francisco trembled, lest this sudden change had caused the poor girl to lose her reason.

"No, no, Minnetta, this is a gipsy camp. Your home is with Don Francisco Alvarez, your good friend, and Isadora, and all those who love you in Logrono," said the cavalier, soothingly.

"Logrono!" echoed the gipsy girl, "Oh, that is a long way off, I think," and she counted her fingers, as if reckoning the distance thither. "Six leagues, I heard them say."

"True; but I can easily guide you there," continued Don Francisco, gradually rising to his feet, so as not to surprise her, and drawing close to her side.

"Who are you?" she asked, as though suddenly remembering herself. "Are you a gipsy, and counsel me to leave this band? I fear you are a wolf in sheep's clothing."

"Hush, Minnetta," he continued, laying his hand upon her arm, "do not be alarmed, do you not know me, do you not recognize the voice of Don Francisco, Isadora's father, and your friend?"

"I do! I do!" she said, trembling, and covering her face with her hands, as she said so.

"Come then, will you not, away from these people, and let me bring you once more to our home?"

"Is this another part of my strange dream —am I still sleeping?" said the poor girl. "I woke this morning, as I thought, from a dream—Oh, a dear, delightful dream!—that had seemed to me to be of years in duration. I dreamed that I had left this mode of life, that I had made new friends, dear, good friends, that they had instructed me—had clothed and fed me; but I looked down to my dress —it was the same as the rest of the band, and I felt that I had been dreaming. But now you talk to me as though my dream were no dream—as though it were all a reality. Are you Don Francisco, and am I your adopted child, Minnetta?"

"Indeed, indeed, yes, Minnetta. That fearful woman must have drugged you when she brought you away from us. But there is no time to lose—come, I pray you, let us away at once."

But still the gipsy girl lingered, and Don Francisco saw the same strange aspect stealing over her features once more, as he laid his hand again upon her arm, and urged her away as quietly as possible.

"Come, Minnetta, come, we are unobserved now—let us away at once?"

"Can I leave this place and this people?" she said, as though she doubted her own power.

"Oh, how I feel that I am a gipsy!" As she said this her whole body seemed to tremble.

It seemed to Don Francisco as though he could not persuade her to leave the spot. Her feelings were so wrought upon by some secret power, that her will was enchained. Suddenly there burst upon his mind the memory of a certain rite that he had years before seen practised by the tribes, and which had doubtless been performed upon Minnetta. *It was the infusion of blood!* A strange and heathenish means employed by the gipsies, of intermingling the tide of their lives, and of binding them together in a strange brotherhood of blood.

When a child is a year old, and the parents desire to inoculate it doubly with the gipsy spirit, so that no association in after life shall separate it from the life and habits of its forefathers, they open the flesh of its arm, and, by a wooden tube, infuse therein the blood of another full-born gipsy, who has been true to the life and spirit of their league from childhood. The wound is then healed by being securely closed and bound together, and the blood thus mingled in the system of the child, is believed, on philosophical grounds, and indeed experience is said to have proved it true, as in Minnetta's case, to so impregnate the system. as to imbue it, in part, with the spirit of him from whom it was taken.

We say Don Francisco suddenly recalled this practice among the tribe, and pushing aside the loose dress Minnetta wore, he found upon her arm, in the usual place, the very mark that indicated this strange rite to have been performed upon her. He saw at that moment the fit was still upon the gipsy girl, and yet there was not one moment to be lost. What should he do? He saw, by her flushed face and full eyes, that the blood had a strong tendency to the brain, and that, doubtless, was acting thus upon her will. His good sense at once suggested a temporary relief, and touching the distended vein in the armpit with his dagger's point, the blood flowed from the wound in a small steady stream. Every moment the face of the gipsy girl grew more and more natural, the eyes resumed their natural expression, and in but little more time than it has taken to tell the story, the entire current of her system was changed from its violent pressure upon the brain, and she stood before him the same gentle and loving Minnetta that he had known in his own halls.

Taking the kerchief from his own neck, he bound up the arm securely, with a dexterity that early and frequent familiarity with wounds had taught him, and felt that a fearful weight was off his heart.

"Now, Minnetta, will you away with me before these people awake and discover us?"

"Oh, yes, no matter how quickly. Oh, signor, take me away from here."

Don Francisco had pursued the gipsies that day nearly the whole way, upon a stout and well-trained mule. The animal he had fastened hard by the camp, where he could easily find him, and hurrying Minnetta towards this spot, he mounted her upon the mule, and urging the animal forward, turned their faces once more towards Logrono. He was pretty sure that the escape of the gipsy girl would be discovered soon after their departure—indeed he wondered that they had not been interrupted in the camp; therefore every moment was most precious to him, as it would divide the force which he would be obliged to contend against. How he longed now for a couple of the fleetest horses that his own stable would have afforded! But leading the mule, he walked forward at a quick pace, each moment placing a greater and greater distance between him and the gipsys.

But they were soon after him; for the watchful Myram, discovering the absence of Minnetta, gave the alarm, and mounting her bravest follower upon the only mule at command, dispatched him on the road they had taken that day, and bade him bring her back at all hazards, if he found her there, never once suspecting that foreign aid had been afforded her to get away. The truth was, as soon as Minnetta awoke from the stupor induced by the powerful narcotic administered to her by Myram in Don Francisco's house, she found herself among the tribe, and wearing a dress like that which she used to wear, and believing herself to have been crazy or dreaming, as she had explained afterwards, when Don Francisco urged her to flight from the camp, had remained so supine that Myram deemed it unnecessary to watch her closely, and thus she had been allowed the liberty that had at first so surprised him, when observing her from a distance.

Half the camp were dispatched in various directions to seek for the missing girl, but he who had gone back on the road they had passed that day was the only one who was likely to see her.

This man happened to be one of the most determined of the band, and he understood pretty well the affair upon which he was sent. It was the same man who, with Rio, had borne her from the house of Alvarez, on the night of her abduction to the camp. He pressed on with his mule and came up with Don Francisco, or rather in sight of him, before they had gone half a league on their way. The cavalier saw that he must now settle affairs by a hand-to-hand conflict. This he cared little for, so long as there was but one enemy to contend with, and once possessed of another mule, he felt sure of making good their escape. So bidding Minnetta hurry forward on the route she was then passing, he paused to confront the new comer, who drew up his animal strangely confused.

At first he could not understand the cavalier's disguise, and took him for a gipsy like himself; but Don Francisco was not one to lose time by idle words, so drawing his sword, he attacked the gipsy at once as soon as he dismounted. The man, though well armed, was no match for such an arm as the cavalier's, and soon received wounds that rendered him no longer able to stand. But as Don Francisco was approaching the mule to mount and follow after Minnetta, the

gipsy, who was evidently dying, rallied, and with one wild effort of determination, staggered to his feet, and aimed a blow with his knife at Don Francisco's breast! The knife reached the shirt of mail, and snapped into a dozen pieces, while the gipsy fell a corpse at his feet!

Mounting the animal he had thus gained possession of, the cavalier soon after overtook his charge, and without fearing any other pursuit, knowing that the band had no more animals to ride after them; and just as the bright morn broke over hill and plain, Don Francisco and the gipsy girl entered the gates of Logrono.

CHAPTER XVIII.

Don Francisco's household—Hernandez and his father's vow—Gay scenes in the city of Logrono. Preparations for the tournament—Queen of Beauty—The contest at arms—The unknown knight—The victor.

"They fought like brave men long and well."—HALLECK.

IT will be understood, therefore, that Don Francisco had hardly been missed from his house, before he returned again, bringing back Minnetta, whom the gipsies had stolen away.

The story of this affair was kept within their own circle, by particular request of Don Francisco, as he had reasons of his own why he particularly desired to keep the adventure at least away from the lips of gossip. As to Signora Alvarez, she was almost beside herself with rage at the failure of her plans to get rid of Minnetta, and yet she was forced outwardly to appear as pleased as any of the household at the gipsy girl's return.

The event only clothed Minnetta with fresh interest in her protector's eyes, and caused Hernandez to love her all the more tenderly for the singular vicissitudes that had befallen her from childhood. The propriety or impropriety of their intimacy was forgotten, at least for a period, and no one wondered at the intimacy of the two when the singular circumstance of her abduction and return was remembered—that was sufficient excuse, for the time being, for any familiarity. At least, Hernandez thought so, and, spite of his father's vow, was almost constantly by the side of her he loved so dearly.

The excitement attendant upon these events had also brought Isadora and the secretary together again. It will be remembered that they had parted with the purpose of meeting

no more. Even Leman Louvelle saw that this was by far the best plan for both himself and Isadora. He reasoned truly and philosophically, that however much he might love her, yet the great disparity in their relative positions would even be a stumbling-block in their way, could he by any chance hope to call her his wife: though as to this, he never for a moment thought of the possibility of their marriage.

At such moments he would say to himself, "Oh, that Heaven had cast her lot in as humble a sphere as my own; how I could love and cherish her, and how happy I could be in life with her by my side as an equal and as my wife."

But in Hernandez' case, the thoughtless ardor with which he met and associated with the gipsy girl was destined to a sudden check. —He found after the first few days subsequent to the adventure already described, that he was hourly growing more and more devoted to Minnetta in his heart, while his father's fearful vow rung in his ears! On her part, Minnetta was only too happy in the consciousness of his love, though she said nothing even to Isadora.

In illustration of a common principle of our nature, the more Hernandez pondered on the stern opposition of his father, the more resolved he felt to carry out his purpose in relation to disclaiming all right to Isadora's hand. He had no one to counsel with—he dared not talk with Minnetta upon these matters; for to her he had only one tale to tell, and that was of his unalterable and earnest love, reading his answer from her eyes rather than from her lips.

The spirit of chivalry was at its height among the noble youths and cavaliers of the district of Arragon, and there had been a lordly tournament announced, to take place in the open plain, towards Anjou. Already had extensive grounds been prepared and properly enclosed, and the necessary fixtures erected to serve in the noble contest for precedence in arms, that was to take place before all the nobility for many leagues around. The tournament was the only theme of conversation for weeks, and the preparation for it seemed to employ every one. Among the fair signoritas there was much surmise upon whom should fall the honored post of Queen of Beauty, to whose share it would fall to award the laurel wreath to him who, by his prowess of arms, should be declared the victor of the hour.

When at last it was declared that Isadora, the fair and beautiful daughter of Don Francisco, had been chosen to the honored station, not a cavalier in Logrono but approved and rejoiced at the choice, declaring that an honor conferred by her hands would be redoubled in value, and that a fresh incentive would be thus imparted to them, as each one would feel the hope that his might be the fortune to win her smile and receive the token from her hand. Hernandez, in common with the rest of the young cavaliers, prepared himself, not so much for the sake of the prize, or to win the smile of the Queen of Beauty, but simply to vindicate his name and credit as a knightly character.

The Gipsy Girl was the only queen he could acknowledge, but she would be present and sit beside the queen of the tournament, and that would be incentive enough for him to do his best to win the honors.

The streets of Logrono were full of strangers from far and near, the hostelries were full of grooms and horses, hurried hither and thither in their gay liveries, jostling each other at the street corners, and laughing and joking in the open squares. Never since the city had received its papers of incorporation, bearing the broad seal of Castile, had it been the scene of so much bustle and noise, as just previous to the grand tournament.

The gipsies, too, had thronged hither, and dancing-girls were challenging the admiration of the gaping crowd, and jugglers were mystifying scores at a trifling charge each. Here and there a crafty Jew was seen making his way among the motley crowd, and even a few Moors might be counted among the throng, though these latter were few, for the Spaniards looked upon them with jealousy and hatred, and never failed to seize upon the least pretext to imprison or slay them. Now passed by some daintily dressed little page,

with his silken doublet and gold-hilted dagger, and now some tall, stalwart man-at-arms, half clad in armor, with his skull-cap of Milan steel, and rattling spurs upon his heel.

The appointed day came at last, and the tournament was one bright scene of beauty and chivalry; noble lords and stately dames lined the arena,—flags danced merrily from the various stands, representing the house of those knights who had entered for the contest, —heralds, with their trumpets, were ranged on either side, and upon a raised pedestal, at one corner of the grounds, sat four grey-haired men, knights sent by the king as umpires, to settle all doubts that might arise as to any precedence, or rights of the tournament, and to see that all was conducted on the true principles of chivalry.

In the centre of the grand circle of spectators, in a temporary alcove, erected with oriental splendor, sat the Queen of Beauty, Isadora Alvarez, supported on one hand by Minnetta, on the other by one scarcely less beautiful. All eyes were turned towards this point, until the heralds sounded their trumpets and announced the names of the contending knights. Among them was that of Hernandez Montedore, and when it was called, the tell-tale blush upon the cheek of the gipsy girl betrayed her feelings; but there was no one there to notice this, and the heralds continued the roll of names to the end.

At last there rode forth into the list a knight upon a proud, milk-white Andalusian steed, who threw down his gauntlet, and challenged any noble like himself to battle. His challenge was at once taken, and a knight, bearing the cross upon his shield and crest, and mounted upon a highly caparisoned horse, rode forth and confronted him. Each made the circuit of the list, bowing gracefully to the assembled beauty, and then took their stands at opposite extremes of the ground. At a signal from the heralds, they dashed forward with lances poised, and, bracing themselves in the saddle, met midway. The knight of the cross was shaken in his seat almost from the saddle, and he who bestrode the white charger lost his helmet.

Again they turned and dashed across the list, at each other; this time he who had lost his helmet before was unhorsed, and severely bruised in the fall, and the knight of the cross was declared the victor. The rules of the tournament were, that he must meet the next challenge, or indeed any that would confront him, if he would be considered to win the laurel wreath, and be crowned by the Queen of Beauty And therefore, after slightly refreshing himself and his horse, his gauutlet was thrown down, and he was ready to contest the list with any and all.

The knight of the cross, who seemed to be proof against all harm since he had been shaken in his saddle by his first adversary, though he had met five others and unhorsed them, remained himself unharmed. Indeed, he seemed to grow better fitted for the contest at each renewal, and twice already had his esquires brought to him fresh horses, and the universal voice declared that he would be proclaimed the victor. He was of large and powerful frame, and showed himself possessed of sinews of iron, and the endurance of a true and stalwart soldier.

Those who had not entered the list, now refused to do so, as they were not willing to risk the mortification of defeat, by encountering one who seemed invincible, and it appeared evident that he of the cross would be the victor of the day, when Hernandez Montedore bade his esquires to announce him; and he rode into the arena, and confronted the successful knight. The challenge was accepted, and the combatants took their places. At the flourish of trumpets they started, and meeting both midway, the crash was fearful. The skilful knight was again shaken in the saddle, and Hernandez bent to the back of his horse by the blow of his antagonist's lance, which he had received upon his shield.

They turned, after reaching the opposite points of the arena once more, and their horses were again in full career against each other, when Hernandez's horse tripped on a spear point, that was left upon the ground, and both rider and horse came to the earth. The knight of the cross rode gallantly by, and, returning, offered his aid to the discomfited cavalier, who, he declared, had given him the hardest bout that day. Hernandez was too much hurt for riding again, at least for some hours, and was led from the list amid the cheers of the throng, who had witnessed his stout and well-directed effort against one who seemed to be more than a match for any one that could be brought.

And still the knight of the cross rode gracefully around the list; a fresh and spirited horse had been substituted for the one he had just ridden in the contest with Hernandez, and the heralds cried aloud his challenge to all. But his success had frightened the timid, and his gauntlet lay upon the ground untouched.

"Now, by the Virgin!" said Don Hernandez Montedore, who felt keenly his son's discomfiture, though all could see how bravely he had borne himself.

"Will no one of better tempered skill and more coolness meet him?" asked Don Francisco Alvarez; "by my sword but I would have donned my armor had I foreseen this. Stay, what noise is that?"

As he spoke there was a slight confusion visible at the entrance of the list, when a knight announced himself; but as he gave no name and offered no proof of his knighthood, the heralds refused him entrance. The umpires discussed the matter, and at length, at the request of the challenger, who said he would waive all considerations of rank, the new comer was admitted within the circle of the list.

All eyes were turned upon him, to see who was so daring as to meet the stout and skilful knight of the cross, who had unhorsed so many. The new comer rode into the area upon a horse of fine proportions, rather strong than handsome, but of fine mettle and action. The knight himself wore black armor, and there was no device upon his shield; but his bearing and manner showed that he was well accustomed to the use of arms. Before commencing in the arrangements for the contest, he stipulated that he should in no event be compelled to remove his visor, but that whether successful or otherwise, he should remain as he came there, unknown. This was acceded to by the judges.

The two knights took their stands, he of the cross with his splendidly caparisoned steed, and the unknown with his coal-black horse and armor, when they awaited the flourish of trumpets that should be the signal for them to dash across the list and at each other. In no contest thus far was there so much interest shown as in this. There seemed at the first glance so much disparity between the two, for the unknown was much slighter in physical development than his antagonist: though those well versed in the game saw by the mode of his handling his horse and the style in which he bore his arms, that he would be no mean enemy; and so thought the knight of the cross.

The horses seemed to know the signal as well as their riders, for they dashed off at once, meeting midway. The lance of the knight of the cross was directed at the breast of his antagonist, as had been his former efforts against the other; but his new adversary had profited by observation, and had discovered his mode of attack, and by rightly placing his shield and suddenly turning its surface, he cast off the force of his opponent's blow, and at the same time changing the direction of his own weapon from the breast to the helmet, he struck it full beneath its trench, and lifted the rider from his horse to the ground, when, dashing boldly on, he thus completed the contest in a moment.

It had been skill, not strength, that had conquered. The unknown returned, and offered his aid to the prostrate knight, who, however, was not seriously hurt. He promptly acknowledged that his antagonist's skill was too much for him; but that when strength alone and ordinary practice was required, he felt himself equal to any other. It now drew near to the close of the tournament, and the time for the Queen of Beauty to crown the victor. But the unknown modestly declared that the knight of the cross had won, by his many contests, the prize, while he had only perhaps by chance succeeded in winning a single one at that late hour.

But neither the knight of the cross nor the judges would admit this plea, though they besought him to make known his name, that they might justly honor one who had been so skilful as to conquer him who had so easily conquered all before that had couched lance against him.

Amid the pageant and martial music arranged to render the scene as imposing as possible, the judges led the unknown to the feet of the alcove or mimic throne where Isadora sat in virtue of her office, and then formally delivering their opinion in the style of the olden times, they bade him kneel to receive the laurel wreath.

They stepped aside as he approached and knelt before her, and in the speech of a few words, prepared for the occasion, she crowned him as the victor of that proud and knightly scene. As she ended, he lifted his visor so that only she could see his face. It was the countenance of the secretary, Leman Louvelle!

CHAPTER XIX.

Logrono after the tournament—A fearful pestilence overspreads the city—Its effects upon the sufferers—The Gipsy Daughter's remedy—The poison discovered—The spy—Preparation for defence.

"Ho, treachery! my guards, my scimitar!"—BYRON.

THE excitement attendant upon the preparations for the tournament, and the gossip that had naturally followed upon the events that we have related, had drawn the eyes of the citizens away from the contemplation of any ordinary matters, and even Don Francisco Alvarez had forgotten his late adventure with the gipsies, at least for a while. Taking advantage of this state of the public mind, Myram had not hesitated once more to return to the camp ground near the city springs, and once more had pitched her tent upon the spot. Her anger at the loss of Minnetta knew no bounds, and on examination of the events attendant upon her escape from the camp, she felt satisfied that she had been aided by some powerful arm, doubtless that of Don Francisco himself.

She saw that the noble cavalier, with his prompt daring and real bravery, was now the equal to all her tricks, and that she could hardly become revenged upon him in any ordinary way, still she was resolved upon vengeance, let the consequences be what they might, and no matter how many were involved in the result. To confirm herself as to Minnetta's whereabouts, Myram sought and met Signora Alvarez, and from her learned that which satisfied her upon the subject of Don Francisco's agency in the gipsy girl's return to his halls.

The strangers had nearly all departed, and the excitement of the late tournament and the festival that followed it was over, when a voice of sadness and woe reigned in the usually gay city of Logrono.

A peculiar sickness had broken out, unlike most others—it did not appear by slow degrees, but at once appeared in full violence in the shape of a terrific and mysterious epidemic. Dizziness in the head was the first symptom; then convulsive retchings, followed by a dreadful struggle between life and death, which often terminated in favor of the grim destroyer. The bodies, after the spirit which had animated them had taken flight, were frightfully swollen, and exhibited a dark blue color, chequered with crimson spots. Nothing was heard within the houses or in the streets, but groans of agony. No remedy was at hand, and the power of medicine seemed to be gone, since those taken with the malady received no benefit from any prescription. And thus the terrible pest had raged in the devoted city for nearly ten days, with fearful fatality.

Thus far the family of Alvarez and that of Montedore had escaped the pestilence from some cause that they could not understand; and Don Francisco, whose studious habits and large experience had made him somewhat acquainted with the power of medicine, had been active day and night in his attendance

ISADORA'S VISIT TO THE SECRETARY.

upon the sufferers, and had met with more success than any others in subduing the disease that prevailed. So great was the fear of contagion that people kept their houses, and few stirred abroad at all, and, governed by the prevailing spirit, neither Minnetta nor Isadora had passed the gates of the house for many days.

On the tenth day, at midnight, Don Francisco was aroused from his sleep by a message imploring his attendance on a neighbouring family, where several women and young children were seized with the pestilence. Minnetta overheard the message, and hurrying on her dress, was in the corridor as soon as Don Francisco.

"You are going to those people, signor?" she asked, meeting him there.

"Yes, Minnetta. This is a fearful scourge, and it is the duty of us all to assist one another."

"Will you let me go with you?"

"You, Minnetta?"

"Yes. Why should not I go as well as you? These women may need a woman's care."

"This is true; but you must observe one thing, Minnetta—neither eat nor drink of anything."

"I will not: but do you think this pestilence is poison, that you warn me thus?"

"I know not; but none of us have yet suffered, and we have neither eaten nor drank from home."

Thus saying the two proceeded together, on their melancholy duty. It was the first time the gipsy girl had been brought in such close proximity to the disease as to observe its effects upon the sufferers, and she marked well every symptom with a keenness that showed a natural skill in medicine. But could you have seen her then, you would have marked a wild expression upon her handsome features, and some strange fancy or stern reality was operating upon her mind. Throwing aside the medicines that Don Francisco had brought with them, she ran hastily out into the moonlight, and gathered a weed that grew rank about the corners of the houses and in the gardens, she gave the leaves of it to the sufferers to chew. It acted upon them like a charm; and the agonizing pain was almost instantly relieved by the patient's consuming only a few mouthfuls of the leaves, chewed finely and then swallowed. It was a specific.

Don Francisco regarded her movements with amazement, and drawing her to one side, asked:

"Minnetta, what means this miraculous remedy? How is it that you so readily understand the disease?"

"Don Francisco, have you never heard of the gipsy poison so dreaded, called the *drao?*"

"Strange," said he, "I know the poison well, but had forgotten its effects, it is so many years since I saw its operation. The *drao!* Then the gipsies are here, and have done this," he continued.

"It must indeed be so. It is the water they drink, signor," said Minnetta.

"I see it all. I see it all—and there is work for me to do. These people are relieved. Let us away."

Thus saying, Don Francisco returned with the gipsy girl to his house, and from thence at once to the proper authorities, to stop the flow of water from the springs into the city. His own house was supplied from a spring within his own grounds, as was also that of Don Hernandez Montedore, and some others of the nobility; and this, if his supposition was correct, was the reason why he and they had escaped the epidemic. When he communicated his suspicion as to the impurity of the water, he said nothing of the gipsies; for he determined to make sure of that first, and should it prove true, to make a terrible example of the tribe he suspected of this dreadful deed.

This first step taken to prevent the spread of the fearful poison, Don Francisco did not wait even for the morning. He was too impatient to delay, and donning the same disguise that had so effectually served him once before in the rescue of Minnetta, he turned his steps towards the spot where he knew the gipsies were encamped, if they were in the neighbourhood, near the springs that supplied the city.

Minnetta by this discovery was thrown into the most painful train of thoughts. She attributed the vengeance of the gipsies entirely to herself, and was sad and unhappy indeed to think she was the cause of so much misery and unhappiness to innocent people. Poor girl! she little knew of her patron's early history! She little knew that he was bound by initiation and fearful oaths to the gipsy league, or of the relationship between him and Myram. It was not the gipsy girl, but her protector, that so aroused the hate of the revengeful gitano.

Don Francisco found, to his surprise, that there was not only the band over which Myram was the leader encamped in the environs of the city, but there were also several others, here and there, upon the hillside, with their rude encampment about them. The cavalier computed them all, with his practised eye, at some four or five hundred. Their proximity to Logrono in such a body, argued no good purpose, and it was evident to his mind that some move of more than ordinary importance was about to be attempted, and doubtless it had some connection with the present plague that they had brought upon the people of the city by means of the poisonous *drao*.

His plan was already adopted. He must mingle with them under cover of his disguise, and by conversing with them in their peculiar language and idiom, discover their designs, let them be what they might, and, if possible, at once take measures to frustrate them, if they involved evil to the citizens, which was the case beyond a doubt. Slouching his hat over his eyes, and putting on a rough, lounging appearance, he sauntered in among the gipsies. Now and then he was addressed by this one or that, but returning an indifferent answer in their own tongue, he was unsuspected, and passed on, gathering what information he might as to their purposes from what chanced to meet his eye and ear.

At last he came to Myram's camp, and here he found gathered the leaders of all those who were encamped about the hill-side, and stealing close to their circle, he threw himself upon the ground, and listened to the cold-blooded counsel and plan that they had nearly matured for the destruction of the citizens.

"Brothers," said Myram, "it is time that a blow should be struck for our race in Spain; the government has long enough hunted us like wild beasts; besides, there is much booty to be had in this gay city—gay, forsooth! I should call it sad since we cast the *drao!* for a voice of lamentation is going up from every street and nearly every house. There is, too, another reason why I wish for the coming fray, and that is, to revenge myself and tribe upon a recreant member of our band, once our leader, but now the proud Don Francisco Alvarez, who also retains in his house the favorite of our troop—the dancing girl Minnetta. What gipsy would not pour out his blood freely for revenge on a recreant traitor to our league?"

Don Francisco was no coward, but as he lay within hearing of that voice, and saw the effect of the words that Myram uttered upon the fierce and reckless spirits that crowded about her, he felt how completely he was at that moment in their power, should they chance to penetrate his disguise. We say he was no coward, but yet a thrill ran through his frame as he considered the critical character of his immediate situation.

There were three points that told well upon her auditors in Myram's short speech. First, her hearers had all felt more or less keenly the rigor of the government authorities, as exercised against their race, and therefore heartily seconded the idea of impressing those officials, by some united and vigorous movement of their power. Secondly, the cunning suggestion relative to the fact that the city would afford them rich treasures in the way of booty, was an idea that acted like a charm upon a gitano; and thirdly, they were bound by their league, and the most fearful oaths, to revenge themselves upon any one who should ever prove recreant to their fearful brotherhood; and thus, although Don Francisco heard the gipsy queen boldly advocate an open attack at daybreak, on the day after to-morrow, on the citizens, yet he saw nearly all the leaders gradually assent, and finally agree to participate in the enterprise.

"But," said one more cautious then the rest, "we are but a handful compared with the whole number of the citizens; and should they defend themselves bravely, we might come off second best."

"Nay," added Myram; "you do not remember the *drao*; you forget that one-half of Logrono is at this very hour under its almost certain poisonous effects, and that a round number lie already in the chapel and convent yards."

"True, there is something in that; but we are hardly four hundred, and they can muster ten times that number, doubtless, even at so short a notice to defend their homes."

"Not at such a time as this. The whole city is in mourning—the pestilence, as they call it, has disheartened them—they feel as though they were all to die, and the poison is still working. Every draught of water that they drink between now and the hour of attack is in our favor."

Don Francisco stayed only long enough to hear them mature their plan as to the attack at daylight on the day after to-morrow, and to hear his own house given out as the rendezvous of all at the expiration of the conflict, when he carelessly rose and sauntered away towards the borders of the camp-ground. But there was the eye of one upon him who knew his step, or thought that she knew it. It was Myram, and she called out at once, "A traitor—secure him!" pointing to the retreating figure of Don Francisco. But it was night, and too dark at any great distance from a person to distinguish him. The cavalier, however, heard her, and turning behind a tent, came out on the other side; he then turned his steps, so as to cross the camp in another direction, or, in other words, he doubled upon himself, putting those who followed him at fault.

He heard the noise and bustle attendant

upon an alarm, running from one encampment to another, as he escaped from their boundary, and taking an unusual path towards the city-gates, he was soon within the walls. As he passed the dilapidated gates, he could not but regret that they had no soldiery to defend the walls, and that they had been permitted, through neglect, to fall gradually into decay and ruin.

His first act was to have a large quantity of the weed that Minnetta had used gathered at once, and administered to those who were suffering, while the rest of the town were warned not to use the water that came from the public aqueducts, but to supply themselves from the few private sources afforded in the city. The courts of Alvarez and Montedore were at once thrown open to them, in order that they might procure pure water. The effect of these measures was perceptible in a very few hours, though the ravage had been so great, that nearly all were on the sick list.

Don Francisco and Don Hernandez, with their dependants, numbering some sixty able men, were at once placed in a state of active defence, by being carefully armed, and the followers drilled by young Hernandez in the part they were to play in the attack on the coming morning, while the authorities—albeit there were but few that were not ill, too ill to act in their official capacity—got together such other citizens as they could find able to bear arms, and a few feeble efforts were made at organizing them for the sudden emergency. As to the small company of soldiers—scarcely a hundred in all—that were kept in commission by the king's orders, the *drao* had swept away one half of them, and the rest were sick.

This was the state of affairs in the city of Logrono, and facts proved that the gipsies had not miscalculated as to the effect of their fearful poison, but had chosen a time for the attack when the place was comparatively defenceless, and quite at the mercy of the weakest force that should put it to the sword.

CHAPTER XX.

The gipsies preparing for the assault—The secret armament—The surprise—The battle with the gitanos — Vivid scenes of conflict—The gipsy queen—The death-bed !

"It was a dread, yet spirit-stirring sight."—SCOTT.

IT was not quite daylight on the morning subsequent to the closing scenes of the last chapter, when the gipsies filed down the steep sides of the aqueduct hill, and quietly approached the city walls. They came in a confused mass, as their leaders attempted to enforce no sort of discipline among them; but a natural instinct kept them as silent as the invisible arm of authority might have done. There were over three hundred of them, all told, and their weapons were as various as their habiliments and individual appearance.

The incident of Don Francisco's partial discovery while he was acting the spy among them, during the council that had been held at Myram's tent, should have taught them to fear that their plan was already discovered by the supposed spy; but the fact was, that Don Francisco had so effectually evaded them by his adroitness, that it was concluded by all, save Myram herself, who was almost sure that she recognised the movements of one long known to her, that their alarm was un-called for by any reality.

But while the gipsies were advancing thus upon the town, there were mustering within the broad court-yard of the house of Alvarez between two and three hundred men, well armed, and under such discipline as to enable them to operate in perfect concert. Among them were many who had either personally suffered by the murderous *drao*, or who had perhaps lost those united to them by ties of blood, through its poisonous effects. Such were eager to be placed face to face with their enemies, that they might be avenged for the foul wrong they had received at their hands; and Don Francisco, seeing the small number that he should be obliged to rely upon, took advantage of this spirit to render his little band more earnest and determined.

Knowing that the gipsies would far out-number the effective strength that he could muster against them under the existing circumstances, and at so short a notice, Don Francisco, who had unanimously been chosen to head them, resolved, instead of meeting them at the walls, to surprise them in the large square before his own house, as he had heard that it would be the first place attacked. The surprise, too, would be more complete and effectual, to fall upon them after they had been led to think themselves unsuspected, by passing peaceably through so many streets.

This was the state of affairs as the grey of morning broke faintly from the eastward, and the light of early day began to struggle, as it were, with that of the moon, which was yet high in the heavens, as though it had tarried over the city to be an eye-witness of the struggle between the contending parties. The gipsies were silent, as we have said, but their heavy tread soon fell upon the ears of Don Francisco and his followers, who now prepared to meet him.

The feelings of Minetta at this crisis can be better conceived than expressed. She was aware of all these proceedings, and their import, and knew full well that the preparations she saw going on were for the destruction of those people with whom her childhood, and, indeed, nearly four-fifths of her life had been passed. It might be that she entertained no particular regard for those persons individually, but there were many associations hanging about her early life, that made her feel now most keenly for the race that she had belonged to. She could not but feel that one word or signal from her might put them on their guard, and prevent the intended surprise; but would not this endanger, perhaps, the life of Don Francisco, the only protector she had ever known? Thus the gipsy girl reasoned, as she hid herself in the darkness of her chamber, and awaited the result.

Isadora, finding herself alone in this fearful emergency, now joined Minetta, and together they sat trembling there by the side of the bed, speaking not one word from very fear for those they loved. Hernandez, and even the secretary, had each been entrusted with separate commands, with directions to fall upon the rear of the gipsies at the same moment that Don Francisco should throw open his gates on their front; and the reader may imagine how Minetta thought of Hernandez, and Isadora of Leman Louvelle, at such a time.

At last the moment of the conflict was announced to them, by the simultaneous shouts of the hosts of combatants on both sides. Then, as Minetta, by far the most spirited and brave in reality of the two, covered her face with her hands to shut out the noise of the conflict, Isadora approached the battlement window, and taking a position where she could overlook the square where the fight was commencing, looked down upon them with an irresistible impulse, though her heart beat so quickly as to be almost audible in the room. One or two observations from Isadora as to the contest without was sufficient to arouse the gipsy girl to listen.

It was not strange that she could not bring her mind to look upon a scene of bloodshed between two contending parties, when she found it impossible in her heart not to think of both as her friends. Though her heart went with Don Francisco to the fight, yet there was a tender regret that his arm was to be lifted against the gitanos. It was more than a simple regret, for the fearful ceremony of the transfusion of blood had not lost its charm—the same fire danced in her veins still, and perhaps she even feared to tempt its power by looking at the fight!

"Oh, fearful sight!" exclaimed Isadora; "my father is lost in the melée, and there comes Hernandez. He falls upon their rear, and—and—ah! how he strikes those gipsies down—the blood flows—"

"Is *he* harmed?" asked Minnetta, trembling; "whose blood flows?"

"The gitanos—the gitanos; he fells one to the earth at every blow!" The fair girl held her breath almost as she gazed, and her tiny hands clasped with convulsive force the sill of the battlement window.

"There, there comes Leman and his followers!" she continued, with startling energy. "Oh, Holy Mother! how they fall upon the gipsies! Leman is in their very midst already, sweeping his sword like a scythe."

"See you Hernandez again, dear Isadora—where is he now?" asked the gipsy girl.

"I see him not—ah! yes, there he is, contending with a stalwart man, a fierce gipsy leader. There! Oh, Holy Mother, his sword is broken—he is defenceless!"

This was too much for the gipsy girl to bear tamely. She sprung to her feet with clasped hands—she looked at the window and at the door, while there was that in her eye that told how promptly she could use her own tiny dagger, were she on the spot at that moment. She seemed hardly able to restrain her feelings

"Quick, Isadora! how is it now?"

"The gipsy and Hernandez are both down!"

"Well! well! can you see them still?"

"Yes; the gipsy rises."

"And Hernandez—Hernandez?"

"He, too, is up again; and, oh! fearful sight, his dagger drinks the gipsy's heart's blood!"

"Thank God, he's safe!" said Minnetta, rising from the floor as though she had not strength to stand.

"The gipsies fly," said Isadora, "all save a few, who crowd about a tall form, one of our cavaliers, who is contending furiously with them—four are upon him, and one is a *woman!* Holy mother! that cavalier is my father—the woman strikes at him with her dagger from behind. See! see! Leman's arm has stayed the blow, but his own blood flows from the wound! Ha! the woman strikes at my father again, and again Leman's arm interposes! A sword flashes over their heads —see! see! they fly! 'Tis Hernandez— Leman and my father are standing safe by his side."

"And the gitanos, where are they?"

"Sad sight! they strew the ground with their dead bodies," said Isadora, with a shudder.

"The woman—is she large and tall?"

"Yes."

"Is she gone too?"

"No; two of our people have her, and lead her this way."

"That must be Myram," said the gipsy girl to herself, thoughtfully.

The scenes which Isadora had thus reported to her companion from the window that overlooked the contest, were a fair picture of the fight between the gitanos and the people of Logrono. Her eyes had been rivetted on one or two points of the fray only, but those represented the whole fight; and deeds like those we have described as performed by Hernandez, the secretary, and Don Francisco, were imitated by their small band of followers. The gipsies, accustomed to rely mainly upon cunning and adroitness, rather than upon any strength of their own brought openly to bear upon their enemies, had sunk almost at once before the well-concerted and united plans of the attack and surprise that had been arrayed against them by Don Francisco and his followers; but being desperate, taken in rear and front as they were, they fought furiously, and out of the hundreds that entered the city gates that morning at daybreak, scarcely threescore made good their escape again from its wall, and many of these were sorely wounded.

The streets of the little Spanish city presented a fearful sight that day, and the groans of the dying echoed fearfully upon the ears of the inhabitants. Grey-haired friars, and sisters of charity from the neighboring convents, offered here consolation to the dying, as they bound up the wounds of the sufferers. The emblem of the cross was offered to the gipsy who was breathing his last, but with averted face he died in his own secret faith. It was a solemn and fearful scene, scarcely exceeded by the late frightful pestilence that had swept off so many of the peaceable inhabitants.

When Isadora recalled in her mind the late startling scene that had engaged her observation, she remembered the marked anxiety that Minnetta had exhibited for Hernandez during the fight. At the time she thought nothing of this, but now that she had leisure to review the scene, it seemed suddenly to open her eyes, for the first time, to a fact that she had not before suspected with regard to the gipsy girl's heart. It was singular what a flood of counter feelings this discovery created in Isadora's heart — she hardly knew how to entertain the idea that Minnetta should love him, who was betrothed to her, and perhaps had already won his heart. At first she was half-vexed, but then she remembered her own love for Leman Louvelle, and she said within herself, "I care not, so he be true to me."

As has been intimated, the gipsy queen Myram was conducted to the house of Alvarez, where a comfortable apartment was provided for her. This she much needed, for her eagerness in the fight had caused her to receive more than one chance wound, some of which were of so serious a nature that the old friar of the house, a man well skilled as a leech, told Don Francisco that she could hardly survive them. A vital part had been touched, besides which the gipsy was very low from the great loss of blood which she had experienced.

It was a singular position of affairs, that Myram should be there under Don Francisco's roof at such a time—come, as it were, to die. The cavalier sat in his study, and mused upon the strange fortunes that had brought the present position of affairs as they then appeared. He looked back, and remembered Myram as the young and beautiful, though reckless gipsy girl he had loved in the mountain passes: he remembered her as his wife, as she who had sold him into slavery; he remembered her now as he passed all those scenes before his mind's eye, and then pictured her attempting his life in his own apartment, where he then sat, and afterwards in the fearful evil she had brought upon the city, the battle itself, and now of her weary body, lying racked by pain under his own roof!

Such were the thoughts of Don Francisco as he sat there alone on the evening of that eventful day.

In the meantime, Myram lay in a half conscious mood, with an involuntary groan escaping from her now and then. By Don Francisco's request, Minnetta, who had desired to attend her, avoided her presence, but the kindest offices were performed for her by gentle female hands, and her sufferings alleviated as far as possible. To the suggestions of the priest she turned a deaf ear, and bade him, if she must die, to let her do so in peace.

Once she asked him how long she should live, and being told, gave a quiet assent to her fate, be it death or otherwise ; but she whispered to the priest to send Don Francisco to her before death had sealed her lips for ever.

"Will you not confess to me ?" said the priest kindly, "and unburthen your mind of the weight that oppresses it ?"

"I confess to no one," she replied ; "were I in the open air, I would breathe my wrongs to the God of nature—no one else."

If the gipsy had any religion or reverential belief, it must have been confused and undefined. Her people performed certain rites to the green hills, and the skies above them, but scarcely had they any definite idea of a God, or of any responsibility to a higher power than the bonds of their own league of brotherhood.

The priest, despairing of the hope to bring the gipsy to any religious sense as to her responsibility to Heaven, bore her message to Don Francisco, desiring his attendance upon her before her death.

"Is her death inevitable ?" asked the cavalier, who could not but entertain some feeling of pity for the woman who had cost him so much misery.

"It is ; and from her mood, I think, perhaps, she may confess to you if you should ask it, for there is evidently some matter weighing heavily upon her mind, of what import I know not."

"I will see her then," replied the cavalier, "though it will cost me fresh unhappiness—for you must know, good father, thaat I have been with this woman under far different circumstances."

"Indeed ! then are some of her half incoherent exclamations explained, for she has been wandering in her mind this afternoon, and has called upon your name at times in singular connection with herself."

"Let secrecy seal your lips, good father ; there may be that in this matter that I will confess to thee ere long ; but at present we must heed her mood, and render her last moments as calm and peaceful as possible."

Thus saying, Don Francisco signed for the priest to leave him, and after walking his own apartment for some moments in silence and thoughtfulness, he turned his step towards the bedside of the dying gipsy.

CHAPTER XXI.

Minnetta and Isadora—A secret divulged—Hernandez and the gipsy daughter—Leman Louvelle and Isadora—Signora Alvarez in her element—The declaration.

"Marriage is a matter of more worth
Than to be dealt in by attorneyship."
Henry VI.

IT will be remembered that Isadora had marked well the earnest feelings that the gipsy girl had shewn for Hernandez during the fight, and that this demonstration of feeling on her part had at once betrayed to Isadora a truth that she had not before even suspected. She resolved at once to seek her confidence upon the subject, for more than one reason—the principal one of which was, that she, too, was similarly situated as it regarded the secretary ; and moreover, she desired to assure Minnetta of her cordial acquiescence in the affection she entertained. In this spirit she sought the gipsy girl, and after introducing the subject with the adroitness of her sex, she said—

"Minnetta, I have discovered a secret, one that I have been stupid not to perceive before."

"And what is it, Isadora ?" asked the gipsy girl, with assumed indifference.

"Why, that your heart is not your own, Minnetta," answered her companion.

Minnetta answered not, but her eyes rested on the floor, where she traced figures with her foot.

"Silence gives consent," said Isadora. "Well, Minnetta, I too have lost my heart."

"I know it !"

"You know it ?"

"Yes."

"Who told you so ?"

"My own eyes."

"Indeed !" said Isadora, now a little disconcerted in her turn.

"I have loved you too well, Isadora, not to observe the workings of your heart, and I have long known that you loved—"

"Who, Minnetta ?"

"Leman Louvelle."

"And you, Minnetta, love Hernandez ?"

"Ay, more than that !"

"More than that ? What do you mean, Minnetta ?"

"I may trust you, Isadora ?"

"In anything."

"Hernandez is my *husband!*"

It would be difficult to describe the astonishment of Isadora at this discovery. She was mute for a long while, musing within herself upon the effect this must have upon those concerned, for she knew full well the proud spirit of Hernandez' father, and was not without fear from that of her own parent. She could see nothing but trouble in future for them both, and wondered when these singular events would finally terminate, and to what effect.

It was even as the gipsy girl had said. Hernandez, knowing well that it was impossible to obtain his father's permission to such a union, and indeed knowing as well that Don Francisco himself would never give his consent to an arrangement that must thwart his own cherished hope, as it regarded perpetuating his name and fortune, even though he loved Minnetta so tenderly—Hernandez had persuaded her to kneel with him before the good friar, who was in his confidence, and with a holy invocation, the priest had married them.

Minnetta had not been easily persuaded to this end; but she loved Hernandez so dearly, that his wish became her law, and to his earnest entreaties she had yielded.

Hernandez knew very well that his father would keep his vow most religiously; and to prevent so rash a deed, there was but one way left open to him, and this Minnetta and himself had already agreed to adopt. The late contest and sickness that had reigned in Logrono had for a moment diverted them from their plans; but within a few days they were to leave the city secretly, and seek a home in some quiet place, remote from the bustle of the world, and securely hidden from the knowledge of his parent and Don Francisco.

No one, save Isadora, even knew the circumstances of the marriage, except the priest, as was presumed, and the gipsy girl could not refrain from trusting her whom she had learned to love like a sister; but as it regarded her proposed elopement, that was known only to Hernandez and herself.

That very evening, Don Hernandez Montedore sent for his son to meet him in his study, and there told him that the events of the few past days had shewn them how uncertain life was; that he was himself already aged, and not a little infirm; that now the pestilence was stayed and the gipsies defeated, he desired that matters between him and Isadora might be brought to a close, and they would celebrate their late deliverance and victory by a marriage ceremony, that should be gorgeous and splendid beyond anything that had been known in their native city. He told Hernandez that he should then feel content and happy; but his son looked as though such a result as his father proposed would render him anything but happy. Still he was forced to acquiesce seemingly in his proposal.

Hernandez left his father with an aching heart. He felt that he must see him no more, and that before the morrow's sun should sink in the west, he must be far away from his boyhood's home. He loved his stern and brave old parent, but he loved his gipsy wife more dearly; and as he turned away from him that night, he stole to a secret meeting with her who was now to him all in all—ay, more than the whole world beside.

As he entered the court-yard of the house of Alvarez, he met Don Francisco at the foot of the stairs that led to the broad corridor. The cavalier was on his way to the bedside of Myram, the gipsy queen. He paused as he met the eye of Hernandez, and offering him his hand, said—

"I should thank you for the gallant aid you afforded me to-day."

"Nay, signor, it was a simple duty, and cheerfully performed," replied Hernandez.

"Our victory was complete, but only owing to the bravery of yourself and others."

"Received you no wounds, signor, in the fray?" asked Hernandez.

"None of import; but you look sad and pale, Hernandez—now I look again, sadly out of humor. What has crossed thee?—art suffering from some sore bruise taken in the fight!"

"No, signor; truth to say, I am not very happy," replied Hernandez, with a sigh, and half longing to open his heart to Don Francisco, for he knew how well he loved Minnetta.

"Cheer up, my friend," said the elder cavalier; "I go on a melancholy errand—to visit the death-bed of one of our late enemies, a gitano. Heaven speed her soul!"

"Amen!" said Hernandez, "if any of them yet live; but I had thought that few, if any, could have escaped the rout of this morning."

"There is one in yonder chamber, the queen of one of the most powerful tribes that were engaged against us to-day. She is dying now, and we must be merciful."

"Is she a tall, athletic woman, that you speak of?" asked Hernandez.

"She is."

And was found engaged in the melée?" continued his young friend.

"Yes."

"Then it was she that I saw twice attempt your life with her dagger."

"Indeed!" mused Don Francisco.

DEATH OF THE GIPSY QUEEN.

"Yes; and but for Leman Louvelle, who received her dagger point both times upon his arm, you would must assuredly have died by her hands upon the field."

There was a moment's pause, in which neither spoke; after which, Don Francisco, raising his eyes from the ground, as he had stood musing to himself, said, with an attempt at cheerfulness—

"Its all past now; that was in the heat of the fight, you know, Hernandez."

"True, it was," said the young cavalier, as they separated on their different missions.

While Hernandez seeks the side of the gipsy girl, and Don Francisco that of the dying Myram, we must turn to another room in the house of Alvarez, where lay one wounded and weak from the loss of blood.

It was the secretary, and by his side sat Isadora, bathing his fevered brow, and whispering kind assurance to his heart. Leman was only weak from the immediate loss of blood. His wounds were comparatively slight, though they bled freely, and he only required a brief period of quiet to be once more thoroughly reinstated in his physical strength and health. This was the second time that he had served the house of Alvarez, at imminent risk on his own part; first, in Isadora's case, on the cliff side, when he had so nearly lost his own life, and now by receiving those dagger wounds meant to take his patron's life. Isadora had been reminding him of this, as he lay there upon his couch, and a faint smile lighted up his pale face as he heard her sweet voice in his ear, and saw her face beaming with the full bent of its tenderness into his very eyes. At that moment Leman forgot his pains, and all was paradise before him.

Ever alive to mischief, Signora Alvarez crossed the corridor about this period in search of Don Francisco. Her countenance seemed to show that she had news to communicate to her noble lord, and so indeed she had; and as he was entering the apartment where the gipsy lay, she laid her arms upon his.

"What would you?" demanded Don Francisco, somewhat sternly, for he was in no idle mood.

"I would see you alone for a few moments." said Signora Alvarez.

"Another time will answer; I am engaged now—an hour hence in the library."

"You should know what I have to tell you instantly—but have your own way."

"Of what import is it?"

"Concerning Minnetta."

"Minnetta is all very well; and I know that you often unnecessarily concern yourself about her."

"She has played thee a trick that will convince thee how little she deserves the confidence you have reposed in her, or the kindness she has received under this roof."

"Indeed! but I know thee too well, and I will not believe that—"

Here a groan from within the sick room interrupted him, and he turned away and passed within the apartment where the gipsy was lying, while Signora Alvarez was left by herself without.

The truth was, she had in her prying watchfulness discovered, and even interrupted, a part of the ceremony relative to the gipsy girl's marriage to Hernandez; and delighted at the chance thus afforded to create trouble, she had only waited for the most favorable moment to divulge the secret to Don Francisco.

We left Isadora just now by the secretary's bedside. She sat there still. Leman had slept, and awoke greatly revived, and a fresh color had crept back to his cheeks again.

"Have you been sitting here this long while, Isadora?" he asked; "you will weary yourself."

"Nay, it is a pleasure to sit by thee, Leman," said the gentle girl.

"Ah, lady! I almost wish these wounds had been nearer a vital part, for to love thee so dearly, and yet to know that you will never be mine, is far worse than death."

Isadora could only bow her head in silence, while her heart beat sadly. She had already acknowledged to him in the fullness of her affection that she loved him. She could say no more.

"Leman," she said at last, raising her beautiful face, and her dark black eyes resting upon his own, "I have thought much within the last few hours of thee, and of the relation in which we stand to each other. Life is nothing to me if it be not enjoyed with him I love. All else becomes vain and soulless, if the heart be not at ease. I care not for title, birth, home—all these will I resign for thee, and from this hour I will be thine, and thine for ever!"

The invalid could have had no balm administered that would act with such magic upon him as these words had done, and he hardly knew whether he was quite himself. He feared that the loss of blood might have weakened his brain, and that this was but a fancy. But no—there sat Isadora before him, her clear and beautiful eyes meeting his; there was no fancy in this—it was a sweet reality.

It was not indelicate or unmaidenly in Isadora to open her heart as she had done to the wounded secretary, for it was the outbreaking of the long-suppressed current of her affections. It was not a love that had grown up in a day, and ripened in an hour, but it had taken root in her heart when she was scarcely more than a child, and now it had bloomed after years of secret growth—years of suppressed and unexposed ripening. Isadora had yielded to uncontrollable impulses.

CHAPTER XXII

The gipsy queen—The singular reconciliation—A startling development—The revelation—The gipsy's death-bed.

"A death-bed's a detector of the heart:
Here tired dissimulation drops her mask."—YOUNG.

THE room where the dying gipsey lay was dimly lighted; but the rays of the lamp were sufficient to reveal the expression of her dark and now pallid features. She seemed to be uneasy at the sight of the close walls about her, and once or twice raised herself upon her arm, though her strength was scarcely equal to the effort, and looked longingly out at the battlement window, where the moon's rays were shining brightly. Then, with a deep sigh, as though she felt that she was looking upon the silvery light for the last time, she sunk back again upon the couch with a cold shudder shooting through her fevered system.

She seemed impatient, too, at some delay, and tossed from side to side with weary glances, until, as Don Francisco entered, she fixed her eyes at once upon him, and motioned for him to sit by her side. The cavalier did as she desired, but paused a moment before he sat down. As he gazed upon that strange dark face, once more the past flitted across his brain with the speed that thought only can attain. He could not forget that the being before him, however treacherous she might have been to him, had yet once been his wife; and it seemed, too, as he gazed there, that something of these same feelings crept over the wounded gipsy, for the sternness was all gone from her eye.

The heart is not so bad as one half the world would make us believe, and there is no soul in which there is not hidden some of the angel still. The poor sufferer's eyes met those of Don Francisco, and though her body was racked with fearful pains, there was sympathy there; the answering token at once thrilled through the heart of the proud cavalier, for kindness begets kindness; and when the gipsy extended her trembling hand towards him as a token of peace, he held it kindly within both his own, and sat close by her side. The memories of both kept them silent for some time, while their hearts wandered back to their first acquaintance together.

There was little that could be said between them. Myram knew that; she seemed only to wish that she might be forgiven for the part she had enacted; she felt keenly, now that death was so near at hand, that she was the aggressor, and that he had never harmed her by word or deed in his life. But this was not all—there was something struggling at her heart for utterance, and she only hesitated to speak, because she knew not in what way to begin; something that nearly affected them both, that was evident. Don Francisco had met her so kindly, that had there been one hostile feeling lingering in her bosom, it would have vanished at once.

"A few hours gone by, this hand was raised to slay you," said Myram.

"That was in the heat of the fray, when the blood was up, and the fight exciting us."

"True; but you never sought my life, Don Francisco," she answered.

"The past is forgotten, Myram, and I trust we both forgive each other. With you, life is now nearly over—your sands are well nigh run. Can I do aught to soothe your last moments?"

"There is much, very much, that I would say," continued the gipsy; "much that I would try to explain, because I find that, indifferent as I have believed myself, still I would not have you think me, when I am gone, to have been worse than I really was during my life. There might be much said as to the force of circumstances, and the untoward influences that have bent me to the will of fortune; but all is now past, and I trust that I am forgiven."

"You are, Myram. I forgive and will pray for you," said the cavalier, kindly.

"I care not for your prayers, only because you utter them. I heed not your religion. I have worshipped only nature, and to nature I shall return, while this weary body goes to the dust. My spirit will soon take its flight, but only to appear again in some other form,

—as a flower, a green leaf, or perhaps a stately tree!"

"Nay, Myram, you exhaust yourself in talking so much," said Don Francisco.

"Fear not. I have marked my time; and not until the moon sinks below the horizon shall my flame of life be extinguished. It will burn with the lamp of nature, and with that will go out to-night."

As she spoke her face seemed to be irradiated with a prophetic fire.

"There is a reason, unknown to you, why I have followed you so closely—at times impelled by interest, and at times by a spirit of revenge; a reason that, in my blindness, I had resolved never to reveal to any living being; but now that I am so near the end of my varied life, I feel actuated by a different spirit."

"What do you refer to, Myram?" asked Don Francisco, with interest.

"After we had parted so unhappily on the Moorish coast, I gave birth to a child."

"You would not deceive me now, Myram?" said the cavalier, much agitated.

"By Heaven; no!" said the dying gipsy, with an earnestness that satisfied him.

"That child, then, was a daughter?"

"It was."

"And Minnetta is she?"

"No—you are wrong."

"How then?"

"Not Minnetta, but Isadora!" said Myram, emphatically.

"Isadora!"

"Yes."

"That is impossible," said Don Francisco, with startling earnestness.

"I speak only the truth. Isadora is my child, and your daughter!"

"Who, then, is Minnetta?"

"She, also, is your child!"

"Wonder upon wonder! Myram, as you hope for mercy, do not deceive me?"

"The truth only is on my lips," said the gipsy, with steady accent.

"Shew me, then, that these things be so, while you have the strength left to do so?"

"I will," answered the gipsy, sighing inwardly at the pain she suffered.

"Drink of this," said Don Francisco, handing her a reviving potion.

Temporarily relieved by the medicine, the gipsy turned her eyes once more upon Don Francisco, and prepared to unravel to him the mystery of years gone by. He was almost too impatient to listen; but suppressing this earnestness, he quietly awaited the gipsy's own mood, for she was very weak.

"When by chance," continued the gipsy, "I discovered that the wanderer whom we had befriended was a noble of the land, I remembered that he was also the father of my child, and interest, combined with the natural feelings of a mother, drew me to the nearest accessible point to his presence. I made your position my study. I knew when your fair, young, and noble wife was laid in her tomb, and I knew, too, full well when your daughter was placed out to nurse. Nay more—I knew and bribed that nurse into my service. For many months you saw no one, not even the daughter of your deceased wife. This was opportune for me, my own daughter was placed with the nurse, and yours, by the noble lady Casada, was taken into my own tent."

"I see; I see—go on," said Don Francisco, with the utmost impatience.

"My first object in this exchange was to insure to my own offspring a better and happier fate than I could afford her should she remain with me; and my second was, through Minnetta, your own child, to revenge myself for the fancied wrongs I had endured at your hands. The midnight attack upon your house, when you took Minnetta prisoner, will bear witness how closely I pursued this plan, and had I entered then, my purpose was to have robbed the house, and to have slain you, telling you first by whose agency we had been able to enter your gates, and thus inflicting upon you a double sting."

"Oh, how could you have been so base?" said Don Francisco, covering his face with his hands.

"I see it all now," said the gipsy, "as well as thou can'st do, but in my prime and strength I could not do so. Now I am dying. The children I hope may be equally dear to you, for your own sake and theirs. I have no longer any selfish wish—my sands are nearly run; yet I would see the girls ere I die. It would be a pleasure to hear them forgive me, now that I can harm them no more. Isadora I have seen and watched often when she knew nought of my presence, but she is far better off than she would be if I should live. Will you bring them to me, Don Francisco, that I may bid them farewell?"

"I will," replied the cavalier, leaving her for the purpose, while he scarcely knew how to meet either Isadora or Minnetta under the strange circumstances that had been discovered to him. He could scarcely credit the gipsy's story, and yet her words somehow carried conviction with them. Besides which, he felt that the truth or falsehood of her assertion could easily be proved, and in his own mind he was satisfied.

While he left Myram to seek his daughters, she groaned with anguish at the pain that rent her body, but she uttered no word of complaint. Now and then she asked of the friar a drink of water, for Don Francisco had summoned the priest to sit by her side while he sought Isadora and Minnetta. Gradually, however, her pains seemed most mysteriously to leave her, and she lay in a quiet calm, that the priest knew very well was the precursor of her death, but the gipsy only smiled at her release from pain.

Faithful to his own honest convictions, the priest once more essayed to make her kiss the cross, and with him lift her hands and voice in humble prayer to the virgin; but it was to no purpose. She smiled in kindness upon him for his purpose and desire for her good, but gently waved him away. She had grown up in a simple faith, and could not change at that late hour; and the priest could only sigh over her firmness.

"Will he be here soon?" asked the gipsy, casting her eyes to the battlement window.

"Yes; he said he would return at once," answered the priest.

The gipsy's eyes still watched the moon's rays as it gently sunk towards the horizon, and she grew more and more impatient every minute, until at last she bade the priest go seek Don Francisco for her. But the noble cavalier entered almost immediately, accompanied by Minnetta and Isadora, to whom he had been imparting sufficient of the revelation that had just transpired, to prepare them for the scene within the chamber.

The priest retired at a sign from Don Francisco, and left them alone with the gipsy queen.

Here we must draw a veil over a scene that the pen could hardly do justice to, and let the reader picture for himself the detail of that painfully interesting meeting. Let him depict for himself the feelings that must have actuated Isadora, at finding Myram her mother, and also those of Minnetta, at the discovery that Don Francisco was her true father, and herself nobly born. We say that we must leave it for the reader to depict these scenes in their earnestness and singular interest.

But the gipsy was near, very near her end now, and beckoning Don Francisco closer to her side, she said—

"Grant me one request!"

"Anything I can do for thee, Myram, I promise thee freely," he replied.

"Then bury me on the open moor, far away from the city walls!"

"It shall be done, Myram."

"Methinks I can sleep easier, and lie more quietly, with only the blue sky over me."

She held Isadora's hand within her own, and both she and Minnetta knelt by the bedside, while she asked them both once more in a whisper for their final forgiveness, and smiled as they uttered it in soft accents to her ear. Then she extended her hand to Don Francisco, who took it kindly and bade her farewell. It was a sad and impressive sight, the gipsy's death-bed.

In a moment more he felt the grasp that held his hand relax—the eyes closed calmly, the breast ceased its gradual motion, and the gipsy queen was dead!

Don Francisco turned toward the battlement window to hide the starting tear, and he saw that the moon had that moment set. The gipsy's prophecy as to her death was fulfilled.

CHAPTER XXIII.

Machinations of a jealous spirit—The secret of Isadora's love discovered by her father—A proud spirit's struggle—The decision—The end of a bitter heart—War with the Moors—The triumphant return—A happy finale and leave-taking.

"The fame that a man wins himself is best;
That he may call his own."—MIDDLETON.

IN the mean time, Signora Alvarez having failed in her attempt to create fresh trouble by appealing to her husband, now sought the residence of Don Hernandez Montedore. The old cavalier received her, and listened to her revelation concerning his son with perfect consternation; but, as she declared she had seen Hernandez wedded to the Gipsy Daughter in the small chapel-room of her own house, he was forced to believe her. He remembered his vow, and at once and secretly determined that he would keep it religiously, and that his son should die!

"You will remember, Don Hernandez, that I forewarned you of this," said the artful woman, as she observed the bitterness of the old cavalier's feelings at the story she had told him.

"I do remember. You told me of this disgraceful amour," he replied, earnestly, "and

I, too, charged it upon Hernandez; and my oath is registered in Heaven, that if he marry not Don Francisco's daughter, he should die!"

"You would not take his life?" asked Signora Alvarez, with secret delight.

"Aye! by our holy faith, yes; with this good right hand will I slay him if he hath broken my command. I would take his life though it were the last act I should perform on earth."

Impressed with a joy that she could not give utterance to, Signora Alvarez retired to gloat over the trouble that she had just set on foot, and to watch for the misery it would produce to all concerned.

On the day subsequent to the death of the gipsy queen, Don Francisco had returned from executing her last request—that she might be buried on the open moor. He sat musing to himself when Isadora entered. Her step was slow and her face sad, and Don Francisco saw that the discovery which had just been made touching her parentage, had worked this change in her feelings. As to himself, if it were possible, he only loved her the more dearly.

"Come, Isadora, and sit here," he said, motioning her to a seat by his side. "Has the strange story that has been revealed to us rendered you unhappy?"

"Only so far as I fear it may lessen me in your love," she said, tenderly.

"That were impossible, Isadora—you are ever dear to me. But there is still another subject upon which I would speak to you. I refer to Leman Louvelle."

"Well, father," she answered, with a heightened color, but raising her eyes honestly to his face.

"I am told that he has taken advantage of my hospitality to win your affection."

"Never has he trespassed the bounds of strict respect and duty," she answered, quickly. "If there be blame it is wholly upon my side, who have ever possessed the authority to expel him from my presence."

"And he loves you, Isadora?"

"Has not his whole life proved it?"

"True."

"Twice has he risked his own life for you and yours."

"True, again," said Don Francisco, thoughtfully, and then, after a few moments' pause, added,—

"And do you, too, love Leman?"

"Father, yes," said Isadora, her full and beautiful eyes resting upon him as she spoke.

The proud-spirited cavalier rose to his feet, and walked the apartment, thoughtfully. Isadora watched the expression of his face,

she could only partially translate its changing phases. He said nothing for nearly an hour, as he walked there, evidently contending with his inward thoughts, and struggling to master some powerful emotion. Isadora felt that her future happiness was being decided, either for evil or for good, within his breast; and at last, as he threw himself into his chair, wearied by the strange emotions that had actuated him for the past few days, she almost trembled to observe his mood, and to see the big drops of perspiration standing upon his brow.

"Isadora," he said at length, "the secretary shall be your husband."

He had struggled with his pride, and had conquered. The peculiar combination of circumstances that had tended to bring about such a state of affairs, had not been unconsidered nor without their influence, and when he gave Isadora his consent to her union with Leman Louvelle, he was as much surprised at his own decision as she was, but as he drew her to his side and felt her tender kiss upon his forehead, he was happy and contented. He had seen too much of misery and misfortune of late, and had been too intimately connected with the causes that produed this state of affairs, not to be humbled, and to have learned to prize the better feelings of the heart above pride and pomp of station.

Sad was the heart of Don Hernandez Montedore, as he prepared to meet his son and execute upon him the penalty which his solemn vow compelled him to inflict. Aside from the mere fact of this feeling, he saw, too, all his proud hopes as to the continuance of his noble name extinguished, as he supposed, for ever. He met Hernandez at his own door, and bidding him follow him to the hall of the house, here he reminded him of his vow, and calmly unsheathing his sword, the stern old cavalier bade him prepare to meet his fate, for his hour had come.

"But father," said the son, "you vowed that your vengeance should fall upon me if I wedded not the daughter of Don Francisco Alvarez. Did you not?"

"I did."

"Her, and her alone have I married."

"Impossible."

"It is even so, as I will shew you."

"But Signora Alvarez told me she saw thee married to the gipsy girl, Minnetta."

"The Signora Alvarez?"

"Yes."

"Oh, I see, and have long understood the spirit that actuated her. But Minnetta is my wife, father, and she is also Don Francisco's child."

"Legally?"

"Aye! by every law, human and divine."

"You tell me wonders, Hernandez," said the old cavalier, as they both retired together to his study. "I may have seemed harsh to thee, boy, but it was for very love of the noble name you bear, and for yourself."

In her own apartment, in the house of Alvarez, the signora was now alone by herself. She had just heard of the new discovery which annihilated all her deeply-laid plans to render Hernandez and Minnetta miserable. She seemed greatly excited, from anger and disappointment : at times she grew very pale, and then her face was once more suffused with an over-pressure of blood, so that her eyes were painfully reddened. She walked back and forth in the room, and then sat uneasily down again, until it seemed that each moment but increased her vexation. How long this continued it was not known, for she was found by her attendants, at evening, lying lifeless upon the floor, and on examination it was easily discovered that she had died from the rupture of some blood-vessel.

Though all due respect was shewn to her remains, which were honorably bestowed in the family vault, yet she died unregretted by every one, her unhappy disposition having rendered her disagreeable to all.

Some weeks passed before these circumstances and discoveries became reconciled with the feelings of Don Francisco and the rest of our characters ; and, as if more completely to obliterate the events referred to from their minds, a war broke out with the Moors, which called forth, by order of the King, every loyal subject of the district of Arragon, to defend the honor and authority of the Castilian crown. Don Francisco, true to the spirit of his nature, at once girded on his sword, and, followed by Hernandez and Leman, joined the standard of the King.

While their lovers and father were battling with their swarthy foes, Isadora and Minnetta were left alone together in the house of Alvarez. Their love was unimpaired by the change of fortune that had come over them unless, indeed, it might be that they loved each other still more dearly, knowing their sisterly relation to each other. It was well,.perhaps, that Hernandez and Leman had been suddenly called away, to afford them all time for thought, and to become, as it were, familiarised, in some degree, with the new position that affected each and all so nearly.

Kneeling together at night, they besought the Virgin's protecting care over those they loved so tenderly, and that they might be returned to them again in safety, and crowned with honor. Day by day came messages from the camp, and still all was well, and Don Francisco forgot not to mention the gallantry and bravery of Hernandez and Leman—the latter having already been publicly noticed by the King for his daring courage and efficiency on the field. How proud was Isadora to hear this—to know that it needed not rank and gentle blood to raise him she loved, but that with his own good sword he was earning for himself a proud and honorable name on the scroll of his country's history.

It was an interesting picture to see those fair and gentle ones sitting side by side, and talking of those away fighting their country's battles. Minnetta held Isadora's hand within her own, tenderly, and love beamed from her beautiful eyes. At their feet crouched the faithful dog, who looked up in his mistress's face with a love as plainly written in his dumb countenance as it could be expressed there. He was a faithful creature ; no change of fortune could affect him ; he was ever the same patient, contented, devoted follower.

"Isadora, we must soon expect our wanderers home from the tented field. The last courier said that the Moors had yielded, and our banners waved over Anjou and the fine provinces that cluster about it. God speed our noble cavaliers, and bring them safely to our sides !"

"To-morrow, at farthest, Minnetta, we may look for them," replied Isadora.

And to-morrow, indeed, they did come, a triumphant band, crowned with fame for the deeds of prowess and bravery they had performed. Don Francisco pressed his children lovingly to his arms, and blessed them again and again ; and as Isadora received Leman Louvelle's gentle and affectionate salute, she saw pendant from his breast the cross of the noble order of Castile. Her father saw her looking at the emblem of rank and honor upon her lover's breast, and turning towards her, told how Leman had saved his sovereign's life on the field of Anjou, by perilling his own, and how, despite the efforts of a whole squadron of Moors, he had borne the wounded monarch in safety from his foes. That for this eminent service he had been knighted on the field of battle, and was now noble Signor Louvelle.

Pride beamed from the eye of Isadora—pride and love mingled. She made no reply; but oh ! how ineffably tender was the look she gave to the secretary, now wearing the insignia and title of a proud Knight of Castile. She loved him none the better for his brave fortune, but she could not suppress a feeling of pride at the exhibition and public recognition of qualities that she knew he possessed.

As to Minnetta, how fondly did she cling about her young husband's neck, and how dearly and passionately she loved him now. All barriers to their happiness were removed: there was no longer any reason for concealment—he was her own, her acknowledged lord; and as he stood there, tenderly encircling her waist with his arm, she felt that she was happy, and that her lot was indeed blessed.

It was a striking picture, the contrast presented by those young warriors, fresh from the battle-field, pressing, with their steel-clad arms, those frail but lovely flowers! Don Francisco looked on the scene with pride and secret pleasure, for those lovely children were both his own, and he felt intensely how fully and truly they loved him, and had ever loved him from the first,

Before the setting of another sun, Leman Louvelle and Isadora were united, and the house of Alvarez was the scene of delight and quiet enjoyment.

Some there were among the older servants and retainers who had learned to feel the warmest interest in the honor and happiness of the house of Alvarez—that looked back now, and contrasted the past with the present—who followed the varied life of Minnetta, the gipsy daughter, until they saw her when she was now the envied daughter of Don Francisco; and some remembered about the child's being put out to nurse, and understood how it had been changed, and another, Isadora, had been substituted in its place by the artful gipsies—but such also understood that the child which had been substituted was also their master's daughter.

And now let us draw the curtain over the happy finale of our story, and leave those whose pictures we have painted to bask in the sunshine of the quiet and cheerful portion that Providence had sent them, after the vicissitudes of their eventful lives.

Let him, too, who has woven these lines for your pleasure, hope he has not failed to amuse you, and to flatter himself that, as you close the story, you will think kindly of the one whose pen has traced for you the scenes of the Gipsy Daughter.

END OF THE SPANISH GIPSY.

LONDON: W. S. JOHNSON, "NASSAU STEAM PRESS," 60, ST. MARTIN'S LANE.